The Diary of Elizabeth Elliot

A Persuasion Sequel

Joseph P. Garland

DERMODY HOUSE PUBLISHING

DermodyHouse.com

The Cover: *Mary Ellis Bell (Mrs. Isaac Bell)*, c. 1827, by the American artist John Vanderlyn (1775-1852). Available thanks to the Open Access policy of the National Gallery of Art in Washington.
www.nga.gov/collection/art-object-page.98944.html

Contents

I am all anger and anxiousness. Penelope Clay had been my most intimate friend in many ways since before we were compelled to leave Kellynch. I insisted she accompany Father and me to Bath against Lady Russell's express wishes. Now, she has suddenly and with barely a word of regret *or appreciation* for all I have done *for* her or all I have been *to* her—or thought I was—abandoned me and my affections, very soon after my cousin William flew from Bath and from me. If the rumours are true, she has left to be his in London! I can scarcely believe it but I fear it is the fact. As they are both now banished from my life forever, I pray to have no need to mention either of them again. Oh how Anne was clever not to have surrendered to our cousin's overtures as I confess I nearly did before he turned—for reasons I shall never understand—his affections to her.

There. It is done. May they make each other miserable and, God willing, may Father find someone far more appropriate than Mrs. Clay to direct his own affections, as I suspect he might have done with *her*. As I think on it, I ought not to have thought so very highly of *that widow* and I surely ought not to have opened myself to her as I did.

I am here alone. Abandoned. My hopes of being properly solicited by a proper gentleman I fear are fading, as my looks soon will. Yes, Father has maintained his. But he is a *man*. Men can age well. Women cannot. A glance at Lady Russell and her crow's feet is enough to prove this. Anne, once so fine, has long since turned haggard and I fear that I can do nothing to prevent myself from becoming similarly so.

In our stay here, the gentlemen to whom I have been introduced are not nearly as pleasant as are those I have seen in our regular trips to London, but even they seem more interested in *other* women who may not be as handsome as I am. But they are *younger*. I cannot change this. I cannot alter that with each day I am closer to being thirty. I had such hopes for my cousin for so long. For the first time, I actually fear that my life is not to be what I have long thought, and Father has long thought, it would be.

Anne. Suddenly contented Anne. I had never given a thought to envying her and now with her advances and my retreat I find that I am all envy about her. I confess to feeling some anxiety, though, for her. I realise that I have not been as appreciative of her as perhaps I might have been. She never understood how trying it was *to me* to be forced by Mother's death to take on all the duties as the mistress of Kellynch Hall. Lady Russell did what she could to ease the task, but only by experience can one truly understand how difficult it was, especially for a *girl* of sixteen.

Indeed, now that Anne has become attached to Captain Wentworth, I must also look at him differently. I will concede that there was a sort of what I thought was unalterable coldness between he and I, but I am no longer so certain in my initial view of him, particularly in light of what my recent experience has taught me. I hope that his view of me might be altered as well.

He has his twenty-five thousand. I expected, as did we all, that with that small fortune and his new wife, he would be allowed to savor both of them and become a gentleman of comfort and leisure.

Now comes word that Bonaparte himself has escaped his little island prison and anxiety increases each day. Must Britain again devote its men and its treasure to finally put down the tyrant?

Father and I are to travel to Kellynch—as guests of Lady Russell, which I know will be especially difficult for Father—in just over a fortnight for Anne's wedding. Captain Wentworth, however, may now be required to report on board his ship even before then. Surely, he and Anne must be married before he is again afloat. But as each day brings alarming news of Bonaparte's advances, and the collapse of resistance to him, at least in France itself, we must prepare for the worst. "At most," says Father, "our Navy will be intercepting those seeking to run the blockade." He reminded me that it was likely to create opportunities for ambitious sailors like Wentworth—who he has come to admire to some extent. We will see if that happens or even if there will actually be a *war* in the end. Either way, it bodes ill for our plans to return to Kellynch for Anne's wedding.

That is enough to begin this Journal. I am quite alone. It seems a proper time to converse *with myself* in this unaccustomed manner. For now, it is late. I must adjourn to my bed and dream of never having to again set eyes upon two of the most disagreeable people I have ever met.

My optimism for the day proved unwarranted. We are being washed with late winter rain and must please ourselves without being able to set foot outside. If there were anyone worth visiting, I should have borne the weather, but there is not. Lady Dalrymple and Miss Carteret left town a fortnight ago. Anne, of course, is gone to Lady Russell at Kellynch Lodge, where Lady Russell is to aid in the wedding preparations. Captain Wentworth has dropped his anchor—which I assume is proper Navy talk—in Lyme Regis for the time being, with one of those captain friends of his, the one marrying one of the Musgrove girls, though I can never remember which is that one.

Even the Pump Room is just a shadow of what it was not a week ago. So I stay in with Father. He tries to read but seems lost without his Baronetage to peruse. As to that, for my part I am elated not to have to encounter a certain person described as the "heir presumptive" in one of Father's additions to it.

I daresay after I have had my midday meal, I will myself venture to the library and find some novel or other to allow me to pass the time. I would much prefer a turn around the green with its opportunity to enjoy the sight of one or two attractive gentlemen and allow them to enjoy the sight of me. Nobody will be out in this weather so neither shall I.

We are not to go to Kellynch for Anne's wedding after all. It is as I expected. This morning, Father received an express sent from Kellynch Lodge by Anne. Captain Wentworth has been called to duty and is already flying to Plymouth. He has asked her to join him. It seems that the Navy had obtained a waiver for its officers and sailors to be married without all of the formalities, especially of the reading of the banns, before their ships leave port.

I read the letter when Father handed it to me. Anne says she hopes that Wentworth will be safe and that she further hopes that he will take her on board with him, as his sister was taken on board for many a cruise with Admiral Croft. As for the Admiral, Anne says he was far too senior to be called back and will remain in residence at Kellynch Hall.

When I finished reading, Father, who had risen and was looking out to Camden Place, quite cleansed by yesterday's downpour, turned to me and said, "perhaps this is a good thing. I do not know what people would think if I were at Kellynch but not at the Hall."

I believe I agree with him. Much as I would have liked to return to that familiar place, I would find it difficult as well not to be able to be at the Hall. Admiral Croft, I expect, would offer to have us stay there, but that would be even more awkward than sharing in Lady Russell's hospitality at the Lodge.

It does not matter in the end. Anne is to rush off to get married and may find herself aboard a frigate or some other boat rising and falling in the Channel or the Mediterranean and I cannot say I envy her that. I envy her other things. Not that.

Here in Bath, the weather has turned favourable and somewhat warm. I soon will be off to take a turn at a nearby green and maybe I will at least see someone worth receiving at least a nod from me.

Saturday, March 25, 1815

I received a letter from Anne. She has such a fine hand, which I recognised at once from the envelope. In it, she…I will copy it as it is again raining very hard and I feel no interest in returning to the novel whose first lines enticed me but so far has little further attraction.

March 15, 1815

Dear Elizabeth,

I have not spoken to you since I left Bath with Lady Russell. I had hoped and expected to spend some time with you when you came to Kellynch for my wedding, but that will not happen now. So I must <u>write</u> to you. I am to shortly travel to Plymouth. As I told Father, I am to be married to Frederick there and since my letter to Father I have received word that he will take me aboard the fine vessel of which he is captain. He cannot tell me its name—he says it will be forever the HMS Anne to him!—but is proud of it as it is newer and larger—a second rater with three decks and fully ninety-eight guns—than his prior ships. I know that there are many who believe a ship with a woman on board is cursed, but Admiral and Mrs. Croft have, I believe, proven otherwise.

I wish to speak to you, and hoped to speak to you when we were reunited, about circumstances of which I fear I may have played a role. That is about our cousin. Since I left Bath, I learned that so has your companion Mrs. Clay as well as our cousin. I promise you, Elizabeth, that I was as surprised that he took the slightest interest in me as anyone. I was ignorant of his inclination in that regard until it was well advanced. Had I known sooner, I would have done what I could to promote you to him. It is a blessing, I believe, that I did not, now that we and indeed the world have discovered how inadequate and mercenary he is.

I have now gone from Father, as Mary did some years before. He will be in particular need from you as he was in the period after Mother's death and I expect that you will be as successful now as you were then.

I cannot say for how long this adventure with Bonaparte will last. I am assured that I am largely safe aboard a new and large Navy ship, at least should the war arise as it is expected to arise. I hope, then, that it will not be too long until I am back on terra firma. My fondest desire is for Frederick and I to be reunited with you. And Father, of course. And Mary. I wish you to know that I will do all that is in my power to support you and Father even as I set my own course and I hope that in some ways you, as my older sister, will help to guide me.

Anne

I am grateful to read such sweet sentiments. With Mr. Shepherd's daughter gone from my side—and my world!—I must look to Anne more than I ever have. I am surprised, though, to read how sympathetic she *now is* to what was forced upon me when Mother died. That cannot signify now. She is right. Matters are such that I believe Father, with this recent betrayal, will be in need of me as he was when Mother died. I pray, too, that I will be able to support him.

We are anxious about the news that does reach us in Bath about M. Bonaparte. Initial thoughts that his escape would be short-lived and that the French people would see to his recapture proved wildly off the mark. Indeed, with each story that finds its way to us, we hear more and more that matters are going in quite the contrary direction. Bonaparte may actually rule France and may be able to raise an army that will again march across the continent.

We have no fears for our personal safety. He has no navy to do anything about us. There are those who believe Britain must play a role in putting him down for a second, and final time. I cannot say that I agree with that. Nor does Father. It is not our problem and it should be to the Dutch and the Prussians and whomever else might be *actually* threated to do something about it. I do believe though that Anne's arguments, made before the last peace began, that it was best to be rid of him with the allies before we faced him alone, may have some validity. I doubt that Father would even go that far, but as it is not a decision for either of us, all we can do is hope that we will in the end prevail.

Father has taken to sitting throughout the morning in his favoured chair after breakfast glaring at the stories he reads in the daily papers he sends a footman to get, including days old ones from London. He regularly tightens his grip on the poor paper and curses the damn fools, as he calls them, in Parliament and the War Office and even the Palace—but less frequently—though the papers seem to have little *actual* news about what is happening beyond the occasional dispatch from somewhere on the Continent. How much is to be believed, I cannot say, particularly given the discrepancies between the reports. I find my temper better served by ignoring the goings on, expecting that I will hear soon enough of something of significance even if I do not know how it will affect us—and in the further belief that the Navy and especially *HMS Anne* is likely safe.

As Father and I ate our breakfast together in the dining parlour, a footman entered with a letter to him. After opening and perusing it, he flashed it at me and said that we had received quite good news.

"We have been asked to have an extended visit to Lady Dalrymple in Ireland."

He slid the letter to me. It was written in a very small, very neat hand which the signature indicated was Miss Elinor Carteret's, writing on behalf of her mother. Lady Dalrymple, the true authoress of the thing, said how pleased she was that our family had renewed and reconciled our relationship with hers after that "unfortunate miscommunication" of so long ago that she could scarce recall its origins.

"A taste of English aristocracy," she put it, would be most welcome in her fine portion of the Irish southeast. The estate is called Astings and we know from her and Miss Carteret's many descriptions of it that it is in County Wicklow, not too distant from Dublin itself.

Her appeal to our position was enhanced by her appeal, Father said, to our *situation*. He leaned close to me to confess that matters had become quite *strained* even in the relatively modest quarters we have leased on Camden Place. "It would do well for us and our honour," he said, "to have at least some of the burdens on the Baronetcy eased by a stay for a decent period in Ireland."

I believe Father was more astute than I might have expected upon receiving the invitation in the assurance that he would be once again safe in the "bosom of the Elliot family," as he put it. "We shall be able to surrender the lease, and the great expense, here in Bath," he added, as if we had engineered the entire thing!

We are in complete agreement. We will vacate the house on Camden Place and at least temporarily relinquish it in favor of Wicklow.

He asked that I write to Lady Russell with this news, expressing our great and mutual regret for having to leave Bath and thus to create a large gulf between us and that fine lady. He and I expect that she will understand our motivation for the change.

Father is to have our Bath agent handle the details and I do not as of yet know when we will be leaving. But as I doubt there will much of worth to buy in Ireland, I must put my energies towards acquiring in Bath the dresses and boots and various other objects that will be necessary to maintain the honour of our family.

I also expect there will be sufficient capable merchants and dressmakers in Dublin that Lady Dalrymple can recommend.

Father has written to Lady Dalrymple to accept her most generous invitation. Arrangements have been made to terminate our lease on Camden Place. It is rented furnished so we need not worry about the contents. Nor are the servants anything but temporary except for the two or three that we brought from Kellynch, who must be let go. Which will be sad but it is a cost that we must accept.

We will be traveling over several days. Father has spent hours poring over maps to determine the best course for us to take to get to Ireland and the finest accommodations we can enjoy as we do. He suggested that we spend several days at Cardiff along the way but I fear we cannot quite bear the expense of such a pleasant diversion so have convinced him that we should continue on with determination to enjoy the hospitality offered by Lady Dalrymple as soon as possible. He has accepted the correctness—and necessity—of my arguments.

I will not miss Bath, at least at this time of year when so many have vacated it. Lady Russell is long gone and congestion at the Pump Room is a mere memory. There is hardly a single man of any degree of handsomeness let alone any degree of money there or so far as I can tell anywhere else in the town. The evening entertainments and diversions are few and far between and I do not know when I last had a pleasant dance with even a halfway presentable man!

I do have one concern. It is that I found Lady Dalrymple and especially Miss Carteret perhaps overly formal when we saw them in Bath. It was quite appropriate, of course. I hope that being with them at their country house will be more comfortable at least to me when we are guests and not mere visitors and that our close proximity will be pleasant.

We have had a new letter from Anne. It is a nice change from the monotony. She tells us that the need for secrecy as to the conduct and location of ships of the Navy is paramount. So we know little about what she does except that she tells us that she seems to have begun to become accustomed to life as a sailor's wife.

She says she can only say that she and Captain Wentworth's *HMS Anne* is on station somewhere in the Mediterranean. It appears that such a posting provides scant opportunity to capture a prize worth anything. It is well that Wentworth appears to not be in need of particularly more money due to his prior success.

Thursday, April 20, 1815

I received quite a fine letter from dear Lady Russell this afternoon. It was waiting for me on the silver tray in the foyer when I came in from a stroll in the fine spring air on our final day here. I sat in the sitting room with its view out to Camden Place to read it.

She is answering my own letter about our going to Ireland. She is glad for the enhanced familial relationship between Father and me and with Lady Dalrymple and Miss Carteret. She has always maintained the importance of cultivating and retaining such relations. She also wrote that she is relieved that we will lessen the burden on the Baronetcy by eliminating the expense of Camden Place. Of course, she regrets that it might be some time before she sees us again—perhaps when we return to Bath with Lady Dalrymple—as we will be so very far from her, in distance but not in spirit, she assures me.

Finally, she says she expects that I have had some correspondence with Anne but if not that my sister has assured her she is safe aboard her husband's vessel.

It is peculiar, I believe, to suddenly be so distant from Lady Russell. I know how at times she has disapproved of me and some things I have done, but I have never doubted that her greatest concern was for Father and the rest of our family.

Before I retire, I will write my own letter to her, telling her how I, and by extension Father, have always treasured her and the support she has given to the Elliots over the years, especially after the death of Mother.

We have said our farewells to Bath. It is our first night en route to Hibernia and we have not gotten as far as we hoped owing to Father's fastidiousness. It took him longer than it took me to properly prepare for the journey. One would have thought we were to be presented at St. James's Court for all the attention that he devoted to himself when we were just rolling over country roads with nary a decent personage to see as we passed or to converse with when we stopped to eat and to change horses.

Oh how difficult it is to understand the people we encounter as we head west through Wales, seeming to find greater ignorance with each mile we go. When I think people could not be stupider, I discover that I could not have been more wrong, though it is perhaps made worse by the coarse language they speak!

We have been told that we reach the Irish Sea on the morrow and so can begin the final stretch of our journey.

I cannot say that I handled myself in a manner of which I am proud in our crossing to Ireland. The seas were a bit rough and neither Father nor I survived unscathed. But we did, indeed, survive it. Being as it was nearly dusk when we arrived ashore, we ventured to spend our first night in Ireland at what we were told was the finest inn on the coast. I will only say that if that be the case, I have the greatest sympathy for those who stay anywhere else.

I know it is a first impression, but the people of Ireland are quite a brutish group. They are all stopping and staring and pointing at us in our finery. It is as if they have never encountered a proper lady and gentleman before! But perhaps it is just being in a seaside town and things will improve as we continue our journey to the north. I have located Astings on a map. I cannot say how long it will take us. I only hope the roads are better than what we encountered in Wales.

The Dalrymple estate, Astings, is in the Irish southeast. It was explained to us when we were in Bath that it stands a mere thirty miles south of Dublin and when we arrived after traveling through Wales and across the Irish Sea ultimately to County Wicklow, we saw how finely positioned it is. The house itself is not old, though there are some types of ruins along the road as we approached it.

Lady Dalrymple has a very fine drawing room that looks out to the east and we are told that in the clearness of the morning—it was late afternoon and dusk when we finally reached the great house—it offers a very fine view to the Wicklow Mountains.

After we were settled, we sat with our hostess and her daughter in the beautifully laid out drawing room, smelling of a number of bouquets positioned throughout. The fragrance immediately put me in mind of my own little flower garden in Kellynch and I had a moment of melancholia that I do not believe was noticed by any of the others. I soon recovered.

Both Father and I complimented Lady Dalrymple on the fine accommodations, and especially the rooms that were in a wing on the second floor that had been set aside for us.

This was followed by an excellent dinner amongst just the four of us during which Lady Dalrymple promised that invitations would be shortly sent to the neighbouring gentry to come and be introduced to us. I will say that Father was most appreciative of the respect that he was shown by Lady Dalrymple and I told him of my own pleasure at being here.

I am already missing the people who we could visit in Bath earlier in the year and the dinners and concerts we were pleased to attend. This is much like life at Kellynch in some respects but I must tolerate it until we can someday return to our own, true Kellynch from which we have been exiled through no fault of our own. It *is* our fate, though, and we must make what we can of it. At least I can hope to encounter some fine Irish blood and that one or two or even more! might *appreciate* the fineness and delicacy of a well-bred English daughter of a Baronet.

I hope we shall find out soon enough because as we enter the summer I foresee a reduction in the number of entertainments that will be available to us. I am sure, though, that Lady Dalrymple will do what she can to enhance *my* prospects. A trip to Dublin itself is promised!

Lady Dalrymple was as good as her word. We came to Dublin late yesterday. Her house is on the north side of Merrion Square, facing that fine park and not too far from Trinity College and the River Liffey. The house is not nearly so ornate and vast as is the one in Wicklow. It is more like her house on Laura Place in Bath. But just from what I could see as her coach and four neared the house, Dublin is worlds apart from Bath—though far the inferior to London.

The house was prepared for us, and an expensively liveried staff helped me settle into my room, which was a very nice one facing over the green. I hope I will not find the street's noise and odors too uncomfortable. As in Bath, the house is between two others of similar style, which Lady Dalrymple said were less than twenty years old and thus had all of the modern conveniences. Miss Carteret told me that the square itself was only recently established and that she hopes that I will regularly take a turn or two about it once we are settled.

She is a peculiar sort of girl, is Miss Carteret. But I find that she can be quite entertaining. It is a great relief to have someone like her as a daily presence in this strange land. She has not, however, explained to me why there are no suitors baying at her door—or her mother's door I should say!—but as a woman too near spinsterhood myself, I do not dare ask her. She does know perhaps more than I would have liked about the course of my own dealings with a certain supposed suitor—*and supposed gentleman*—who I have forgotten!

In Bath, gossip reaches all places, I believe, high and low. It was such tattle that provided me with the deprived and scandalous news about HIM and another forgotten person I last saw there, news confirmed many times since.

Now that I have seen the square from my window, I can say that I would very much like to take turns around it with Miss

Carteret and thus learn more about her. I daresay I will do much with her, she being the only woman of my situation I know in Dublin. I have expectations that that will change when we are introduced to society here, as Lady Dalrymple has also promised we shall.

It is very late but I must not retire before describing, however briefly, this evening's entertainment at Lady Dalrymple's house. The house is large and narrow. Its drawing room, though, is too small to allow for any true dancing, an activity I understand Lady Dalrymple does not have a particular interest in.

The room is well large enough, however, to allow for a proper dinner. It was an honour to be seated at her left when we adjourned to the meal itself. Father was greatly pleased to have been allotted the place on the opposite end, and Miss Carteret was to *his* left. He and I had been with Lady Dalrymple and Miss Carteret—who I am increasingly thinking of as simply Elinor—to greet the visitors when they arrived, and I can truly say that the condensation of the Irish to him as Lady Dalrymple's near relation has altered his entire view of those people!

It has been many months since I have seen him as aglow and pleased with his surroundings, and I could not imagine he would ever be so outside of Kellynch Hall itself.

A yellow admiral was to my left. To my confusion about the term, he explained, me not being as conversant in naval matters as Anne has long been, that it meant that seniority had pushed him out of being a mere captain but reality left him without any further duties so he was in essence put out to pasture on half-pay. He was a slight, frazzled creature. After he was introduced to Father and me upon his arrival, Father quietly said to me that he was very glad that *his tenant Admiral* was a far superior specimen of a naval officer and I must say that I think much the same. He was all lines and wrinkles with a face the colour of mahogany, rough and rugged to the last degree.

He said to me three or four times that his ship, the *Swiftsure*, had done its duty for England at Trafalgar. "The French had their own *Swiftsure*, you know, in the battle," he said, and I had no reason to doubt him. I surely was not familiar with the Navy's deployments and officers, and Lady Dalrymple stopped him from positioning utensils as we awaited the beef. He wished to recreate his ship's role in the battle but she gently prevented it by saying "much as I am sure Miss Elliot is interested, I am afraid it shall ruin her appetite, such talk of sea battles." I was very grateful for this intervention, although it did leave the admiral sulking, if only briefly. I was able to maintain my part in the conversation when it resumed by referring to my younger sister having recently married a captain who had been called back to duty, an observation that quite pleased my neighbour, though he said he did not recognize the name Wentworth. He did, though, say that he *did* recall a Captain Croft fighting at Trafalgar. I believe we were both pleased by this exchange and the balance of the meal was enjoyable enough.

Other than that, the younger gentlemen were handsome enough I suppose but there were far too few of them and those who did not know her were, I believe, intimidated in seeking an introduction to Elinor by her being Lady Dalrymple's daughter and in seeking one to me because I am the English daughter of a fine Baronet.

I perhaps ate too much and needed some port to settle myself. I was glad I only had to navigate a flight of stairs to get to my room. Still, I expect I will be well enough in the morning to attend services with Father and our hosts. I am told it is a fine church they attend when in town.

The society in Dublin is of some interest and I regret that we are not to remain any longer. Tomorrow we must be off again, heading back to Wicklow.

Sunday services were a dreary affair though. Lady's Dalrymple's church was scarcely as fine as the one we all attended in Bath. It had portions corded off because of debris that had a tendency, Elinor told me in some embarrassment, to fall onto parishioners.

More generally, and perhaps as unfortunately, I must say that I find the Irishmen I have met here somewhat coarse creatures, strutting about like peacocks and very much pleased with themselves. What it is that they have to be pleased with themselves *about* I cannot say. I met not a one who was a match to those with whom we met while Father and I were in London, I will say that. Perhaps it is inferiority they feel for being here and not there.

News from the continent reaches Dublin before it gets to Wicklow. That news, though, is hardly more enlightened than it has been for these many weeks beyond the universal expectation that with Bonaparte now in charge of the French, there will be some resolution and that we and our allies are fully expecting to prevail. How true this is and how much it is more a hope than anything else I cannot say. I cannot believe, however, that with all of our armies we shall not be able to make quick work of whatever group of vagabonds Bonaparte is able to pull together.

Being here, of course, means no news from Anne. I have become anxious about hearing from her. But I hope that there will be a letter or two waiting for me when I return to Wicklow. I believe this is likely because Anne, even on a boat, is a more consistent correspondent than I am. I do find my time stolen from me almost every day in my walks with Elinor and otherwise making polite conversation with Lady Dalrymple. I am fortunate to be able, now and again, to place my thoughts down in this Journal as often as I do. How I am to write to Anne or Lady Russell—or Mary for that matter, though she will not care—with what I am doing I cannot say.

As I prepare to leave, I can look out at the Square. I have walked there with Elinor almost every day except the one on which it rained heavily. It often rains here, but they tend to be brief showers that quickly pass through. I have discovered that Elinor is an intelligent, insightful woman of great wit, though one would never have imagined this to be the case from the encounters I had with her in her mother's presence in Bath and even here in Ireland. I am quite glad of it, and I have told Father so as I believe it is a most natural connexion between us.

He, too, appears to find her at least an intriguing creature. I have happened upon them once or twice engaged in quite intense discussions, the subjects of which I do not know. I cannot say what if anything will come of it, but I can say that Elinor is vastly superior in all respects—other than looks—to a certain widow who I have already forgotten.

Now that we are back in Wicklow, I must reacquaint myself with country manners and to the greatly reduced contacts, even anonymous contacts, with others. So I was quite and suddenly excited when Lady Dalrymple said she has invited and fully expects that we will be joined on the morrow by a gentleman of a fine Irish lineage, who was particularly interested in being introduced to me. My views as to those in Dublin are not flattering but I do have my hopes for such a gentleman in the country. He is apparently visiting some sort of relation at an estate not too far south of Lady Dalrymple's. She says that I will surely find him to be a gentleman of interest.

When I mentioned him to Elinor, she smiled and with a lowered voice said she was not so confident as her mother. She would say no more. We shall see, I suppose. We enjoy dining with Lady Dalrymple at Astings in the usual course but dinners do tend to be somewhat dull affairs so any new blood, particularly the right Irish blood, must be of interest.

I know it is asking much, but I would also like to have more letters from Anne. Who I miss as I did not before she became a married woman.

I will say that if Brendan Bowen is a specimen of fine Irish lineage, I should like to have no more to do with any like him *ever again*. He is an ugly man. Not tall and quite round. His head is red and his hair has thinned so when he stands he appears nearly to be some sort of torch!

A particularly unpleasant odor emanates from his body and radiates all about where he stands. I cannot understand how anyone could *tolerate* it but tolerate it I was required to do as Lady Dalrymple insisted that I converse with him. I will say that I could barely understand him for his accent and the lisp that I imagine was the result of well deteriorated teeth, which he endeavoured to display frequently when he smiled condescendingly at me, Lady Dalrymple, and Elinor, the only women in the room. His favourite, and really *only*, topic was that Irish lineage about which Lady Dalrymple was so enthusiastic, though I found it as interesting as the lineage of some oriental functionary!

I was not saved at dinner. Oh No. It was as I feared after being introduced to him, and he was placed to my left. An elderly gentleman friend of Lady Dalrymple from a neighboring town was to my right. He was stone deaf and had great difficulty using his utensils and provided no respite for me as to Mr. Bowen. I will commend Mr. Bowen by saying his manner of eating was perfectly consistent with his manner in all other things. He assured me several times that he had a large estate somewhere in a part of Ireland well outside of Dublin that I had never heard of, though I did not admit this to him. "It must be truly lovely," I said more than once and he invariably responded that indeed it was, indeed it was.

He is in his early forties, he told me, and his father was nearly on his last legs. "I am the only son, you know," which I did not. I was not buoyed by the notion.

All of this might have been tolerable and I might have been convinced that with some alterations this gentleman could be made somewhat presentable if his estate was large enough and his father was old and feeble enough had I not had the *great misfortune* of finding myself alone with him after we ate and before we all reassembled in Lady Dalrymple's drawing room. This was surely by design in that after I excused myself to care for certain things, I found him waiting for me in the darkened hallway I had to traverse to return to the others.

"My dear Miss Elliot," he said, nearly upon me in a single motion at which, even in the dark conditions, I saw was not in any manner graceful. Even so, it was far more graceful than what ensued for he positioned himself in a most ungentlemanly manner that forced me to back towards the wall. He placed an arm across my head and his hand was on the fine paneled wall of Lady Dalrymple's hallway. *I was his prisoner!!!!*

"I have heard a great deal about you and your beauty."

Had I not been shocked by this statement, I should have collapsed either from fright or from a physical nausea that crested over me with his awful breath. But I did not faint, perhaps kept standing only because he had trapped me against the wall, though it dug into my back.

I was mute as he continued. "I have spoken to your father, a quite admirable man and a credit to society. He has suggested some...difficulties with respect to his...fulfilling his obligations as a baronet. I told him," this odious creature went on in words so remarkable that I have no difficulty recording them with precision, "that I have no such difficulties and would be most happy to provide assistance to him should I be fortunate enough to have him become my father-in-law."

I could not believe him, with his audacity but was even more shocked, if that was even possible, when he said that Father had suggested that this was a most interesting prospect and that he, this odious man, should make his interest and *affections* known to me at the soonest moment.

"And this is the soonest moment, Miss Elliot," he said and I was blessed that there was insufficient light for me to see the smile that I could smell coming from him.

I proved myself stronger than I might have expected, though, when I was able to respond, in a calm voice, that I very much did appreciate his attentions and that I hoped I might have the opportunity to explore them with him at a more...appropriate time and place. I should not have wanted to reflect poorly on Father and wished to speak with him before doing anything that I could not correct.

He stepped away from me and extended his arm towards Lady Dalrymple's drawing room and with a nod I resumed my journey. He accompanied me into the room and all eyes were upon us. I cannot say what he did as he was behind me, but I was proud to have displayed the appropriate smile of the daughter of a fine Baronet and we took to playing cards until it was time to leave. For two hands he, Mr. Bowen, was my partner and we won some trifling amount of money and I recovered some of my spirit by the time I made it to my room.

When Father inquired as we were leaving, I told him that I found Mr. Bowen of some interest, but he was observant enough not to inquire any further on the point.

What I will do on the morrow I cannot say. How I will be able to sleep tonight I cannot say either. I must pray and in the morning perhaps I will better know what I am to do about that man and particularly about Lady Dalrymple's expectations regarding him. And me!

I deeply love Father but perhaps never so much as now. After he had had his breakfast, he came to my room. He has done this when he is troubled. I had finished my own tray and rung to have it taken away. He appeared as my lady's maid left with it.

He asked for my view of Mr. Bowen, and I told him that I found him to be rough in parts. He begged that I speak the truth to him, and I did. I told him that should he wish me to pursue something with Mr. Bowen, I would of course do so but that I found him to be an odious, ungentlemanly man. "I do not know what they take for manners in Ireland," said I, "but it would never be adequate in a proper English home."

Father said he had come to the same conclusion. He denied that he had given the Irishman the slightest encouragement beyond saying how fine I was as a woman and his daughter. As to our financial condition, he must have heard some unfortunate tattle about it. Father said he feared how Lady Dalrymple would react if I was too ready to dismiss Mr. Bowen as a potential suitor.

I told him I will do what I can to satisfy Lady Dalrymple but only to a point. I said I do not know what that point is but it is well short of making any sort of entanglement with him.

Father said that was all he could ask and that he was very thankful that I had taken our family's position with Lady Dalrymple into consideration and that he hoped it would not be overly burdensome for me to continue a sort of charade with Mr. Bowen until we could be free of him, although we do not know how!

I fear I must say more on this disturbing subject later, but for now I wish to enjoy the Wicklow air, which I believe I will take in on my own today.

I have been excruciatingly busy and have neglected writing. I confess, though, that there is little to write about. Mr. Bowen has not been back, so that is something. When Lady Dalrymple makes reference to him, she seems content in me describing him as an interesting man and leaves it at that.

It takes some days for news of the world, and especially of the events on the Continent, to reach us at Astings and when it does we cannot be certain about how true it is.

We are following the news from the Continent as well as we can. In truth, however, there is little to say about that. Our army is in the Netherlands or thereabouts and the Prussians and others are there too.

It is thought—again I cannot say if this is the truth—that Bonaparte has somehow assembled an army as large as our own but whether he would use it to attack or use it to defend, no one knows. No one doubts, though, that something is sure to happen. So we can only wait for the drips of news to reach us in County Wicklow.

As to the Navy, there is little information beyond confirmation that whatever may be said of Bonaparte's army, he has no navy. I take the lack of news, or even speculation, as a fair sign. The press likes nothing more than news of a great sea battle and there has been no such word. Captain Wentworth and Anne must be leisurely—and most boringly—floating back and forth as part of a blockade of some harbour in France, and I hope she is becoming accustomed to life as a wife and as a wife of a sailor! It is a life, being married to a sailor and not simply being married, that I could not imagine myself enjoying. I know ships are kept in fine shape but there is only so much that can be done at sea and particularly on a ship of war. And to only have brutish men for company!

For me, I should like to find myself a fine gentleman with a fine estate in a fine English county—not too distant from London I would hope. I should be glad not to worry that the ground might suddenly vanish beneath my feet!

I will say that such a prospect has become even less likely here in Ireland. Perhaps that will change with my greater exposure to better Irish blood than I have happened upon heretofore.

Perhaps if we return to Dublin, I will be introduced to additional prospects. There are few (and one of those is Mr. Bowen, to whom I have been necessarily polite and no more in his visits to Astings) here in the country. Men with prospects, it seems, find ways to go at least to Dublin if they cannot reach London itself so that all that remain are their fathers and the second or third sons destined to join the army or the clergy.

I did not expect the news to affect me as it did. Elinor and I were taking our usual walk although it was warmer and the air was denser than we expected when we left the great house. There was a sudden and fast, perhaps joyous ringing of the village churches' bells, Anglican and Catholic alike. They did not cease and as we happened to be not far from the road to the house, we hurried there to see what we might learn.

Just as we went through the fence that bordered a field, a rider flew past us heading to the house. I recognized him as the handsome boy who worked at the stables but we could say nothing to him, he sped by so quickly. We got onto the road and started hurrying towards the house, asking each other what it could possibly be. When we were nearly there, the rider came charging back towards us, slowing down just enough as we scurried to the side to say VICTORY! VICTORY! several times before he was gone amid the dust he'd disturbed.

This great news was confirmed when we neared the house after our unladylike! Race. Standing in front, waiting, were Lady Dalrymple and Father.

Lady Dalrymple deferred to Father. He said the official news had just come from Dublin that there had been a great battle and that we, led by the Duke of Wellington, had prevailed and that Bonaparte and his army were all broken up never to bother anyone ever again!

Oh the joy! I could not have known what it did to me, this news. Wentworth and Anne will be back, and I expect they will soon be at Kellynch Hall with the Admiral.

I also feel that *this time*, unlike the last, we are finally done with this war business. I confess that it did not take a particular toll on we Elliots. Yet except for a brief period in the Years Two and Three and just so recently, we were fighting the French—and then the Americans!—for so much of my life. It cannot help feeling joyous to be free of it all, and of the

American dispute resolved some months ago. Peace and prosperity. And, dare I say it? Paris?

That will come, I daresay, but on this day we—Father, Lady Dalrymple, Elinor, and myself—rode into town and there, in the town square, a round of Huzzahs rang out to Lady Dalrymple as we slowly rode through and we too heard *and felt it.* It was a great day, lessened, if only a little, by us being in Ireland and not in England and especially not being in Kellynch, where we ourselves would have been the recipient of the Huzzahs.

Life is cruel in its own way, even on a joyous day such as this one. And I do not know whether I have missed being home, in *our* home, so much as I do today.

This evening, the Monday after the receipt of the great news, Lady Dalrymple had a grand feast. With fine weather, tables were set up much as is done, as I understand it, for the harvest feast when the crops have been brought in in rural counties. I must say that we never had quite such an event in Kellynch. I found the informality and the mixing off putting until Elinor convinced me that time would pass far more quickly if I at least tried to enjoy myself and I admit that this bit of advice was very useful to me. Though I did not touch any of the ales and such that the town folk were splashing all about, I may have had more claret than was advisable. I will also say that however boisterous they were, never did they show any disrespect to their hosts or to Father or me. I did not dance.

I received a letter from Anne this morning. In my current state, I anticipate such letters with an enthusiasm I could not have imagined only six months ago. It carried unwelcome news though. Wentworth's fine ship—the *HMS Anne*—remains stationed somewhere—she says she still may not say—in the Mediterranean and that it could be some months before they are finally home.

She said he suggested that with the war over, she might prefer to sail home on a companion's vessel that *was* returning to England but she immediately rejected this as being the exact opposite of how and with whom she wished to spend her every married day. I wish I could feel such for a man. Someday perhaps I will.

I was remiss in recording this earlier because we are in the early days of summer and it is quite enjoyable here in Wicklow, with the sun not disappearing until well after dinnertime.

The society here is not nearly what it was in Bath. It more approaches that of the country world of Kellynch, although of course we are not the premier family except by connexions to Lady Dalrymple. We have few visitors except Mr. Bowen and others far too ancient to be of interest to me—or Elinor. Of course we have no Pump Room to parade about. Under the circumstances it is passable, if barely, although Lady Dalrymple has promised that we will venture to Dublin again at some point.

I am increasingly pleased by Elinor and by being with her. We now take turns regularly around the estate—as we did in Merrion Square—and sometimes go into the village together. The shops there are barely tolerable and I am grateful to have been able to buy sufficient things in Bath before we travelled here as well as during our too-brief stay in Dublin. But the village shops do provide us with some amusements and it does wonders for my sensibilities to have tradesmen bow down deeply to both of us whenever we enter their little establishments.

But to Elinor. She is far different when she is out of the sight of her mother, as she never was when we saw them in Bath. She is a very clever, witty girl—though she is of course very much a woman—of the sort one sometimes encounters in some of the better novels written by women authors, and not the silly things that seem far more popular. I will admit at least here that I have read more than a few of them and have enjoyed them at times more than I have those created with greater *gravitas*.

We will go arm-in-arm for what seem like hours at a time, the minutes flashing by as we do. I find this somewhat surprising. I was at first horrified by the liberties she took with her words and her opinions on all manner of things. She recalled in crushing detail the characters who visited them in Bath or who were encountered in the Pump Room or on the pavement. I cannot say, in truth, whether she was more brutish to the men or the women in their peacocking, as she calls it—and I will say I felt at least a nick from the rapier she so readily waved about us!

In honesty, I cannot say she was far off the mark in her laughing at me as I am sure she must have before we became truly acquainted like the cousins we are. I hope I am not so absurd now as I believe myself to have been at that long ago time.

She, though, turns into a nun of sorts when in her mother's presence. She barely speaks unless spoken to and when she does she is very careful and sparing—as opposed to sparring!—in her words. It is as if she is two different people and I must say I much prefer one over the other.

I will say that she is properly deferential to Father. She appreciates his role in the family, especially with her own father, the Viscount, gone these ten years. I believe she quite admires Father and he is an exception to her failure or refusal to engage meaningfully with visitors to Astings.

My God! I cannot long dwell on my discomfort with Mr. Bowen, who has visited several times and even walked alone with me once or twice but about whom I have kept from my Journal because of how truly unpleasant this charade to keep Lady Dalrymple happy has been for me.

No. Far more troubling news has reached us. I as usual had a tray brought to me in my room and did not venture down until it was nearly midday. The moment, the very moment that I reached the drawing room with its fine view in order that I might contemplate what I would spend the rest of my day doing, Father was upon me.

"At last," he said to me about being available to him. I did not understand what was so urgent and it frightened me. He confirmed that we were alone and asked the servants on duty to leave us. When they were gone, he led me to a pair of patterned chairs that were set up in one corner, angled to one another to allow for intimate discussion. When we were settled, he removed a letter from an inner pocket of his jacket before replacing it. After a final glance at the door, he turned to me.

He said that the letter was from Mr. Shepherd. The news was quite shocking because it told of Mr. Shepherd having been approached by a lawyer for some of the Baronetcy's creditors. That lawyer said his clients had tired of "waiting, waiting, waiting," as Father put it, and intended to commence some sort of legal proceedings against the estate as soon as the court was again in session, at Michaelmas.

"That lawyer is a most ungentlemanly sort of person and his clients are worse. I should never have dealt with the scoundrels but as they say if one lies down with dogs one gets fleas."

At this, he rose and for several minutes was silent as he paced about the room, pulling the letter out and putting it back several times.

Finally, I could take no more. I asked him quite directly to tell me what *we* are to do.

That got his attention and he was again sitting beside me.

"Do? Mr. Shepherd says that there is not much that I *can* do." He again pulled the letter out and pushed it in my direction. I, of course, wished to have nothing to do with the thing but I took it and gave a quick glance at its legal mumbo jumbo before I lowered it to my lap.

He said that there was an understanding that he would pay off these debts with interest in due course. That he thought it was agreed that it would take some time to reconcile the obligations of the Baronetcy.

He grabbed the letter from my lap and waved it in front of me. "It seems I have most grossly overestimated the integrity of the Baronetcy's creditors." He said that they are now seeking to get judgements against the estate. *Judgements!!!*

I interrupted by asking whether I should go to Kellynch.

"You?" he said. I did not like his tone, I will say now, but I believe it was the anxiousness of the moment. I told him that he certainly could not return like a defeated man. He glared quite harshly at me when I said this, but I placed a hand on his, the one grasping Mr. Shepherd's letter, and it seemed to calm him.

I said he must trust me. "Did I not provide invaluable service after dear Mother died?" I asked. He had to admit that I had. So I said I would do the same, now that I was again *needed*. He said he would ponder what I had said and we would speak about it after eating.

Nothing of course was said about it at dinner. This was, thankfully, an informal meal, as no one else, most particularly Mr. Bowen, was with us. The conversation was much as it always is when we are only the four of us, with the exception of Lady Dalrymple's references to Mr. Bowen and my assuring her that I found him to be a "most admirable gentleman," which I think she believed, though Elinor knows I am hardly being honest.

Thankfully the dinner was brief and no thought of playing cards was expressed when we were done so I found myself alone with Father in the drawing room. He agreed that I would go to Kellynch, and I was much gratified by his renewed trust. He suggested, too, that I consult with Lady Russell. He admitted that he was perhaps too ready to disregard some of the retrenchments that she suggests, which was a position I agreed could not be borne without doing great damage to the family and the Baronetcy, and said as his "ambassador" I might be more open to her suggestions, though nothing was to be done without his express approval unless it was absolutely necessary.

I suggested that we write to Lady Russell and in addition to seeking her guidance with Mr. Shepherd that I stay with her in the Lodge. This was perhaps the only option since I could scarcely spend my time with Mary in her and Charles's Uppercross Cottage, which was the only real alternative.

Father is to write to Lady Russell in the morning and I will include my own short note, expressing my enthusiasm for again being under her tutelage, as I was after the death of Mother. She is much an ally of Anne's, but she cares too deeply for the family—and why never as we all expected *particularly* for Father????—to turn me away.

Lady Dalrymple could not have been more gracious. If she had some inkling of why I was suddenly leaving Ireland and Father was remaining, she gave no indication of it. Father had concocted the story that the letter he had received brought news that a dear family friend had become suddenly and dreadfully ill and that it was a matter of urgency that I, at least, go to her as quickly as possible.

I told Lady Dalrymple and Elinor that I greatly regretted this necessity of my leaving but that I had no choice. They were quite kind in their appreciation of my difficulties, and Lady Dalrymple offered to do anything she could do, sparing no expense, to expedite and make my journey comfortable. And now as I think on it, I cannot say for a certainty that they were entirely fooled by our story.

It happened that there were several additions to our group for dinner tonight, most notably Mr. Bowen. At the table, Lady Dalrymple announced my impending departure to the room, and a wave of sympathy washed over me from all sides.

Afterwards, Mr. Bowen approached me. I expressed to him in the most heartfelt terms my particular regret for abandoning him. I prayed that he not pine for me as my absence might be of a long duration or even permanent. "I cannot allow my misfortune to interfere with your happiness," I said, or words to that effect. He was quite affected by this, and said how grateful he was for our acquaintance, limited in time as it was, and that he would always cherish it. He asked whether he could write to me, and I thought this much too forward and told him that I most regretted that I did not think it appropriate, in what I hope was the most diplomatic manner.

Now that that bit of unpleasantness has been accomplished, I must prepare. I leave for Kellynch near first light. My trunks have been packed and loaded onto one of Lady Dalrymple's finer carriages. Both she and Elinor came to me before they retired, saying they regretted that they would not be up to see me leave but saying how greatly they enjoyed my company when I could give it to them and that they would care for Father quite well when I was gone, with the hope that our friend would recover sufficiently so my return to Ireland, or perhaps to Bath when they returned there, would not be long delayed.

I thanked them and truly felt a great amount of regret that I was being forced to leave them so suddenly and so soon after I had arrived. I have become fonder of the old dowager than I could possibly have expected and even more with her daughter.

I am in Pembroke Dock, Wales. We are spending the night here after crossing over from Ireland. The Irish Sea was much calmer than it was when Father and I went the other way and thus the trip across was more pleasant, and less gruesome, than it was before. It was dark when we arrived, and I was immediately taken by carriage to a small inn not too distant from the pier. It is a most dismal place. A barely tolerable dinner was brought to me in my room, which was perhaps too close to the sea for my liking with the windows having to be open in the warm air. There is far too much of the "sea air" for my taste.

I am being accompanied by a young Irish girl who Lady Dalrymple has put at my complete disposal during my trip, "however long it might take," she said. She is called Bridget and is a short girl who is very pale, somewhat round, and very shy and sweet with scarlet hair and a perhaps unfortunate number of freckles. This is yet another of the kindnesses extended to us by Lady Dalrymple—and further evidence that she may be more aware of our circumstances than she—and Elinor—allow.

Bridget has proved to be a fine companion, at least in her willingness and I believe genuine excitement about reaching Kellynch, never having been more than twenty miles from where she was born. We shall be off in a hired carriage at dawn, I am told, to continue the journey to England and then to Kellynch itself.

The trip to this point has been uneventful. Lady Dalrymple kindly gave me the use of one of her finer coaches with a handsome coachman and one plain and one very handsome footman. I thought the latter was at times overly familiar with me, however. It was amusing I suppose. Always offering to hold my hand as I emerged from or returned to the carriage.

Always smiling more than I thought was appropriate. I cannot say what experience this servant has had with other woman for I cannot speak to the mores and conduct of the Irish but I was most unnerved by it at times, and I thought him a bit of a chancer. It did not work with me, I am pleased to say.

I will confess that were moments, thankfully few in number, when I perceived a glint in his eye that was not entirely unwelcome and would perhaps not have been unwelcome were he a gentleman and a man of substance. I was able to quickly banish such thoughts the moment they arrived but I confess further that they did put me in a bad way. I can still see the glint I perceived in the very fine eyes of the ~~Heir Presumptive~~ HP in that period before his attentions strayed to *my sister*. There have been moments in my loneliness since he, and *her* in the end with him, abandoned our family when I have *felt* a base desire for him, more than I ever did and perhaps ever will again. I further confess to at times having a longing in me for one I once thought was a dear friend, false as I now know it is and perhaps always was.

I should be settled now. My beauty cannot last forever. I have been so blessed in this regard but fear that I have allowed it and me to waste away. I had every expectation when Father and I were in London over the years that I would find my match. Yet while many were those who directed attention in my way, the handsome were not rich enough and the rich were not handsome enough and as I learned from Father it was most inappropriate that I, the daughter of a Baronet, should accept anything less than a man of fine breeding, finer finances, and the finest of looks!

I make light of it now but in truth I cannot, as I wrack my brain, think of any of the men who would have been mine for the slightest encouragement that would have been worthy of my family. Perhaps it was because the HP *was* part of our family, if only recently reconciled to the fact, that I would have been his for the slightest encouragement on *his* part.

Alas, he has proved himself not to have been a gentleman and surely not a true *Elliot*. He will get the title, I suppose, but it will be so tarnished and cheapened by the man wearing it that it will be nothing of value and I fear that I will find myself *embarrassed* by the connexion.

How things and life would have been different had he proposed to me those years before he married that rich but unsuitable woman who I am to understand had no virtues in looks or manner or blood but only in *money*. He was expected to make an offer to me, at least by Father and me, but he refused our invitations and disowned his obligations to our— *to his*—family, and perhaps it would have been better had he never sought to recover them when he became a widower. A *rich* widower.

Perhaps he would have remained a man of good character—assuming that he ever was!—had he allowed me to be part of his life and to nurture him as his wife and dearest friend when we were both so much younger.

These thoughts I must excise. My task is more immediate and more important than my own selfish desires. I at least will act to enhance the Elliot name. I will be Father's ambassador. The road may be long, but we will again be back at Kellynch Hall.

The hired carriage in Wales was not as comfortable as Lady Dalrymple's and the footmen were not nearly so handsome as was *one of* hers, but that did not signify. Once we crossed into England and passed near Bath itself, I knew it would not be long before we arrived. And arrive at the Lodge we—at long last—did.

Lady Russell well calculated when I would reach her. She had not had the chance to respond to Father's request that I be allowed to stay to confirm the arrangement but she welcomed and was well prepared for it.

It was mid-afternoon when we, by which I mean the hired carriage with me and Bridget on board, rolled up to the Lodge. That good lady was upon me the moment I stepped down and her servants were removing my trunks as she grasped me tightly. I will confess that I do not know if I was ever so pleased to see her after my long absence from this place I love so well. The Lodge is not the Hall, of course, but it is so close to it. A mere half mile!

I was more tired from my journey than I expected I would be and I am not so young as I once was so when we were inside, Lady Russell presented me with Sally, the maid who, with Bridget, is to be at my disposal while I am her guest. I was well tendered to at Lady Dalrymple's but this enthusiasm is beyond any of my expectations.

So I was allowed to soak in a tub with footmen regularly carrying the hot water to it while Sally sat nearby clutching a pile of towels on her lap. Bridget was tired from the trip and though she offered to serve me after we arrived, I thought she merited some time to recover in the room assigned to her (with Sally).

I was glad to have the opportunity to speak only to Sally while I bathed. She did not speak at first and was very hesitant when she did. I daresay that being on Lady Russell's staff had not exposed her to one such as myself and I fear that my appearance and my most ladylike manner intimidated her. She is a young, thin creature doubtless from a nearby farm and has a very smooth face and a fine set of teeth.

It was clear that she was not going to speak to me unless required to do so so I decided that I would speak to her. I was particularly curious about the tenants at the Hall. *What were they like? How often did they venture into the village? Who did they visit? Does anyone visit them?*

She informed me that she had not seen them often. Mrs. Croft's brother, the Captain, she said, stayed there briefly not long ago before heading to the Channel coast. Miss Anne arrived at Lady Russell's at the same time. Word quickly got around that he was being called to his own ship and all of the village prayed for his and Miss Anne's safe return after she followed him. She said all the village was aware that they had since gotten married and they were very happy about it.

I must stop here as I have become drowsy and will rest briefly before Sally returns to prepare me to have my first dinner with Lady Russell and only Lady Russell, for many a year.

It has been very long since I felt so intimate with Lady Russell. When Mother died, Lady Russell paid particular attention to me and the new role I undertook as mistress of Kellynch Hall. I was so very young, though I did not think so at the time of course, and quite different, she said, from Mother. I was up to the task, she promised me, of guiding Father in his grief and the emptiness that he felt without her. I did not yet understand how much he had depended on her.

She reminded me of this while we ate. It was only the two of us, and dinner was set in a small room that was on the opposite side of the kitchen from her grand dining room. She said she much preferred this far smaller parlour when she was alone or when she had but a few intimate friends as guests. She said she had many a fine meal with Mother in this room, and it was that memory I believe that led her to go on and on about her.

I did not object to her words, at times delivered like she was removed to some distant time when Mother was alive. I had not appreciated the effort Mother put into running the household and tending to Father's needs. That realization only appeared when that role was forced on me. Not that I resented it. I dearly love Father and understand how important he is. And not for a moment did Lady Russell call that or my devotion to him into question.

It is quite late and I shall wait till tomorrow to think more about this. Mr. Shepherd will be coming to talk to us and I am most anxious for several reasons about seeing him again.

Whatever is the situation with his daughter, I will say that Mr. Shepherd was quite properly condescending towards me and, indirectly, Father. We did not venture to speak a word about the widow, and I believe all three of us—Lady Russell was with us the entire time—were the happier for it.

We chiefly spoke about the cause of my hasty return. Several creditors in London, he said, had conspired with a lawyer there to agree upon a plan for obtaining satisfaction for certain debts owed to them without regard to the impact it would have on Father and the Baronetcy. "They care not for the remains after they picked over the carcass," is how Mr. Shepherd most undiplomatically but honestly put it.

He agreed that such an attitude was abhorrent to any proper Englishman but that these creditors were no gentlemen and were determined to get their money "by hook or by crook."

Mr. Shepherd assured us that nothing could be done for several weeks. This would, he said, give us time to travel to London, where we could retain a lawyer to see what could be done. I had only just finished the journey from Lady Dalrymple in Ireland but that would not signify given the importance of our troubles.

Lady Russell was quick to promise me that she will make the trip with me and we will stay at her house in Mayfair for as long as necessary. Mr. Shepherd will go too. He said he had written to a lawyer who came highly recommended as being able to provide us with the services we will require when we get there.

Knowing that we are to actually do *something* calmed me from the anxiousness that is nearly constant since Father spoke to me about these matters. I do not know how I could have tolerated things were it not for Lady Russell. She is kindness itself, and we took a short turn around her fine and blooming garden with its great variety of colours after Mr. Shepherd was gone.

It was only us two for dinner, and we were again in that small room near the kitchen. We are to leave for London in two days' time and I hope we will be able to resolve things when we get there. I have just now written to Father confirming my arrival here and telling him of our plans—so far as they have been developed—and my letter to him will be off even before Lady Russell and I depart for London.

I am quite pleased with how matters transpired today, the last before our journey to London. It has nothing to do with the financial concerns. Those I have managed to place in the recesses of my mind until we get there. No, we had very solicitous visitors to Lady Russell's!

Father and I had met the Crofts when they came to inspect the Hall. We found them, especially the Admiral, to be of a very good humour and to be most solicitous to Father. I recall that while we were walking, Father said to us all that he believed the Admiral was the finest looking sailor he had ever met and even more that with some slight changes he would not be embarrassed to be seen with the man. I thought the same. Until, that is, I came to see Captain Wentworth, who I must admit is an even finer specimen of a sailor!

I was quite reluctant to go to the Hall, however, until they paid me a visit at the Lodge. And today, that very thing happened. Shortly after midday, a fine but small gig rolled up in front of Lady Russell's. It had a single horse and two occupants, who I immediately recognised as Admiral and Mrs. Croft.

I watched as they came to the house and heard them gain entry with his booming voice rising up from the foyer—I had left my own door ajar for the purpose. When Bridget (who has fallen in well with Lady Russell's other servants) came to inform me that we had visitors and that Lady Russell desired my company, I went down to them.

I will say that the Crofts are kind. As they had when they toured the Hall, they observed the appropriate formalities in our greeting.

They insisted that they were most excited by the prospect of again meeting the seniormost of the Elliot ladies about whom they had heard so much—I cannot imagine from whom! They said they hoped that I would not hesitate "for an instant" in coming to visit them at the Hall whenever the idea struck my fancy. They did warn me that it was often the case that they were not at the Hall because they spent much of their time walking or riding about the neighbourhood, which Mrs. Croft said she found even better than they could have hoped, which, the Admiral said, must be owing to Father's care of the property.

They made a point of saying that they also hoped that when I did come, their treatment of that great house and its gardens would meet with my satisfaction, and that I would so advise Father.

Mrs. Croft made a point of saying they very much wanted my opinion on whether she has treated what had been—and I hope again will be—my own flower garden by the house with the care it deserved.

I will say that being alone with them and Lady Russell was quite satisfying as they deferred to me at every moment and I do believe that they were genuine in expressing their disappointment when the time to terminate their visit came "far too rapidly," as the old sailor put it. They do display a commonness and genuine sweetness of conduct that I found most pleasant.

I am most satisfied with how the Crofts' visit went. As Lady Russell and I leave for London on the morrow, I cannot return it, at least for some time. They have made me anxious to do so promptly upon our return to Kellynch.

I am not pleased with the London lawyer who Mr. Shepherd suggests we retain. He is, according to what Mr. Shepherd has been told, *the* lawyer to see to protect against unscrupulous creditors. His name is Donald Dumpkin and I found it particularly suited him as he is old and corpulent with only a few, randomly-placed hairs on his pocked head. I will grant, though, that he was quite respectful of us when we arrived. He had a clerk bring us into his large office, which was cluttered with books and papers in no apparent order and was very well-lit by the bright sunshine.

When we were safely settled and had declined his offer to have someone bring us tea, he began by announcing that we should be aware from the first moment, *the very first moment*, that his fee would be high and that as with such cases he would require that a third party with ready resources—that is, cash—guarantee payment of his fees and that he would in addition require that a not insignificant sum be placed with his bank to ensure that he would be...paid.

We were all a bit taken aback by his attitude and his insistence that there were many other clients he would be unable to assist if he provided assistance to us and that there were many other lawyers who could assist us if we could not *afford* him. He was all matter-of-fact in this, making it clear that we must *want* to hire him if we could afford it, now and then pulling a kerchief from his sleeve and running it above his mouth.

I looked at Lady Russell, but her eyes remained focused on the lawyer, and she said that she would vouch for her great friend the Baronet and would provide whatever assurance was required to commence working for him, although he had yet to say a word about what he *would actually do* for Father and the Baronetcy.

He thanked her most heartedly and signaled to his clerk to place a document in front of me with instructions that I was to sign it for Father and then hand it to Lady Russell to sign it for herself as guarantor.

"There is no need, Lady Russell, to have the funds delivered before I commence work since we have little time and must not delay," he said, and he doubted most greatly that Lady Russell's banker in town would have any difficulty in transferring funds to his own account, to be held, of course, in escrow against the work he is to perform, "which I hope will be satisfactory"—he leaned forward with his long hands towards me—"though you must understand that I cannot *guarantee* any result and that the road ahead will likely be difficult and very perilous and I need you to understand that and I note that this very thing is stated in black-and-white for you in subparagraph (d) of paragraph 7 of our agreement." He pointed in the general direction of the document.

I scurried to confirm this language and I found it. I looked at him after handing the paper to Lady Russell for her review. I must say he looked at me quite lasciviously, though I cannot say if it was because I am a woman or a potential client. Then as Lady Russell read the document, he said "I cannot perform miracles" two or three times. I heard Mr. Shephard mumbling, "true, true" after each one of them.

We signed the agreement, and he had his clerk witness it and only then could we tell him what we knew and could Mr. Shepherd hand him the relevant documents that he had received in Kellynch.

Mr. Dumpkin looked at them one after the other while we watched his finger move left to right and down a page until he was done with it. Then with a guttural *harrumph*, he placed that page face down to the side on his desk and turned to the next one. When he had read the final page, he banged them all on the desk to align them and centered the stack in the middle of his blotter.

He proceeded to look up at us, one after the other, before his glance settled on me, between the other two.

"Miss Elliot," he began, "it will not be easy." He nodded at me and then at Lady Russell and Mr. Shepherd before his gaze was back on me. He said the situation was precarious, very precarious. It was happening more and more with his titled clients, their becoming overextended with their duties and obligations. It was so, so unfair, but the law can be used very well by those who know how to use it. "And I," he made clear, "know how to use it."

He reached for a gold snuff box that was near the edge of his desk and placed it in front of him. After opening it, he lifted some with a pinch, which he held to each nostril and inhaled before running his kerchief beneath his nose and returning the box whence it had come. He did this very quickly and almost before I realised it, he was speaking again.

"I know the lawyer for these creditors. He *does*, I am afraid, know how to use the law. But he also knows that too quick a victory against Sir Walter of Kellynch would be pyrrhic indeed. We lawyers must understand each other."

As far as I could understand it, he said he would be in contact with "my friend"—by which I assume he meant this other lawyer—with whom he believed he could arrange for Father to be granted some additional time to resolve matters. How he would do that he did not say. What he did do was push his chair back, slap his thighs, and raise himself up, standing stiffly before telling us that he would contact us when he had anything to report, "anything at all," he promised.

With that, his clerk suddenly reappeared and opened the door to his office and before we knew it we were out on the pavement in the sunshine at the front of his building. Mr. Shepherd suggested we go to the right to get a hackney cab to return us to Lady Russell's.

It was such a whirlwind, although this lawyer surely was not, and I do hope that he will be able to do what he says he will do. I have written to Father reporting on what happened and I am sure he will have to agree that we have done what we had to do. I just hope that by the time he actually gets the letter in Wicklow something will have been accomplished here in London.

I also reminded him to be sure to advise his hosts of the condition of the "ill friend" for whom I have come to Kellynch.

We have been in London three days and though we were told that we must not have any expectations of any progress being made in such a short period, I find myself most anxious that *nothing* appears to have been done about Father's and the Baronetcy's situation.

Far worse, though, appeared late this afternoon in the body of the Heir Presumptive himself. Though our presence was not widely known, it appears that our Mr. Shepherd disclosed it to his daughter who, it can be no surprise, transmitted it to the HP.

He appeared dripping with sympathy for our plight, though I know it is *his* plight that alone concerns him. His visit was mercifully brief and we—Lady Russell and I—expressed our greatest appreciation for his expression of concern and prayed that it not cause any upset to him.

And now that he is gone, I can only hope that it will somehow rebound badly for him, provided that does not significantly affect Father's situation.

Lady Russell again admits how wrong she was with regard to that *gentleman* and how wrong to seek to persuade Anne that he was a far better creature and would prove a far better husband than Captain Wentworth would. I fear that good lady is more susceptible to our aristocratic blood than is proper, which is *I admit* a lesson that I have come to learn.

With our lawyer having negotiated a delay in the creditors taking any action against the Baronetcy—I do not understand precisely how it was done but can only say it has, albeit expensively, been done—we may return to Kellynch.

My further letter to Father has already been dispatched to Ireland. I hope he will be satisfied by what Lady Russell and I as his proxies have managed to accomplish.

I am glad to be going down from London. We have been here so briefly and our presence has not been widely circulated that we have yet to attend a single event or entertainment but at this season I cannot imagine there will be many that could be of particular interest to me.

Lady Russell asked if I would like to stay longer, but I have tired of London in only the short period we have been here. I believe it must be all of the uncertainties that weigh on me. I cannot say what will become of me. For now, I will be pleased to finally leave this empty place.

I may have spoken too soon in my last entry. Lady Russell and I are leaving town Tuesday next. This afternoon, however, we had a most interesting visitor.

In some ways, he was quite forward, not having been introduced to either of us. But he defended his appearance in a captain's uniform in a most particular way by expressing himself as a *dear friend* to Captain Wentworth himself and a recent and *dear acquaintance* to Anne!

Anne remains with Wentworth on his second-rater. That ship, she told us in a letter some weeks ago, is on station off Gibraltar—she says they are not so concerned about secrecy as they were—and is being required to remain there until matters on the continent are *finally settled*. She assures us that there are more than sufficient entertainments for her as she is rowed into Gibraltar itself with the Captain so she can wander the town—with a naval escort—while he attends to the business at hand with the Admiralty.

Our visitor is a fellow captain and was on station with Wentworth in the Mediterranean. He, though, had the good fortune of being ordered to sail home and turned on shore at half-pay. Wentworth and Anne, he said, asked that if possible he would visit us and carry with him some things, which most were small items sent for our safe-keeping, from them, and that is what happened. Anne, he said, had received my letter saying Lady Russell and I had travelled to London—though I daresay she did not tell him *why* we were in town, which I had explained to her in broad terms that I am sure she well understood. He took the chance that we might still be at the address Anne had included in her letter.

Our gentleman caller's name is Thomas Marston. Captain Thomas Marston. I believe he is about Wentworth's age. He is quite tall with dark features heightened by the exposure to the sun that Father finds so distasteful in a Navy man. But for him, it complements his features, I will admit, very, very well.

His hair and brows are very dark as are his eyes and his nose quite long and thin. More than anything, though, is the very long SCAR—several inches at least—that plunges down across his right cheek. It seems an old wound, and he gives no outward sign that he is even conscious of its existence.

"Wentworth tells me that I have far too high standards in my search for a wife," he said to let us—*me* I daresay in Anne's never resting mind—know he himself is in want of one—"but I can tell you, Lady Russell, that there appear to be at least two women in this very room who could easily meet the highest standard of the most fastidious of sailors."

Dear me, I thought at the moment, he may be sailing too close to the HP in his use of sweet words and I am determined that I shall not be seduced by what he says.

But notwithstanding that, and in light of the delightful way he carried on, paying particular attention to the remaining vanity of Lady Russell—I believe to put me off his trail—I have decided to keep an open mind about him. We are set to leave shortly for Kellynch, but Lady Russell encouraged him to visit again while we remain in town.

I am sure nothing will come of it. Yet I am not quite as enthused about our leaving town as I believe I was at breakfast!

Captain Marston seems to have thoughts about me that are not so different from my thoughts about him. He appeared today at Lady Russell's. It was a fine summer day without some of the heavy air that has cursed us recently. He suggested that we might take a turn around a small green not three blocks from Lady Russell's house. He *insisted* that Lady Russell accompany us, although she *insisted* that she not. In the end, he won out at *my* insistence, and the three of us had a delightful walk.

As we returned to Lady Russell's, he asked whether he might be so forward, under the circumstances of our impending departure, to solicit an invitation to dinner on the morrow, as he is not engaged. Without bothering to ask me, Lady Russell was quick to extend the sought-for invitation and he was quick to accept it. With that and an exchange of courtesies, Captain Thomas Marston was gone. He seemed to be quite happy with himself, as I must say was Lady Russell.

When we were alone, I assured her that I had not the slightest objection to his proposal and so now I can look forward to one more thing before we leave town.

The contrast with Mr. Bowen could not be greater.

It is quite late, but I cannot retire without recording how pleased I was with our visitor. Lady Russell arranged for one of her London friends, a solicitor who did work for her and her late husband some years ago with whom she continues to correspond and who had already visited us once, to join us for dinner and cards.

The small group and the lack of pretense made for one of the most agreeable evenings I have yet to pass in town and both the Captain and the lawyer proved the equal of Lady Russell in their knowledge and insights and were gracious in including me in all that was being said.

She arranged for me to be paired with her friend while she was paired with the Captain for several deals of whisk from which no one fared poorly and I was sorry to have the time pass so quickly. The two gentlemen left together with regret for the forthcoming departures of Lady Russell and me. But depart we must and I am content with the fine hours I spent today.

The day was quite pleasant and the trip back to Kellynch with Lady Russell was enjoyable. The Lodge was ready for us, and while it is not of course *home*, it does suffice, as it must. We had a small dinner in her little room, and I was glad to sit with her in her sitting room doing needlepoint while she read until it was time for us to retire and plan for the morrow.

With matters having settled into routines, I pine for correspondence, and was not at all disappointed in the mail I received this afternoon. It was from Ireland and Elinor.

Father has been coy about what I have reported to him as it concerns our family's situation beyond expressing his overall satisfaction for what Lady Russell and I have done and accomplished. Elinor made no reference to anything along those lines and merely said she is hoping that my ailing friend is recovering and that it will not be long before I will be able to return to Astings.

I immediately took up pen and paper and wrote back to her, assuring her that fine progress was being made and that it was my fondest wish to be reunited with her, either in Astings or Bath.

I truly wish it to happen. I am very fond of Lady Russell, far more fond than I could have imagined, but she is so much my elder and in a way my *aunt* that I cannot feel she is my friend, at least as dear Elinor is—and as a certain long forgotten person I once thought was. I do see Mary often enough but she is and always shall be *Mary*. Anne will, I am sure, soon be here as well, to my great satisfaction.

For now, though, I survive on letters from her and Elinor and it must suffice in the heat of my August days.

Thursday, September 28, 1815

I today received a letter from Father that is so extraordinary that I cannot possibly do it justice so I will simply copy it down:

Astings House
County Wicklow

September 18, 1815

Dear Elizabeth,

I write with news that I trust you will find pleasant. It is that I have made an offer to Miss Carteret and she has accepted me. Since you departed, she and I have taken to enjoying frequent turns about Lady Dalrymple's property, much as she tells me you and she did before you were compelled to return to England. We even spent three days—with Lady Dalrymple—at Merrion Square and I was most gratified to have her be in my company each time I went out.

During these periods, and at other times during each day, particularly late on a summer evening, I have found her to be intelligent and most appreciative of my position. This, of course, is quite natural given her own position in our family and the high esteem in which I hold her mother and, I believe, in which her mother holds me.

I did broach the subject with Lady Dalrymple beforehand, of course, and she raised no obstacles to it. Indeed, she said it was something that she had hopes if not expectations about occurring. She warned me, however, that the final decision was for her daughter and her daughter alone. She said that she had come to respect and admire me in our frequent and regular contacts since I have come to stay with her.

I felt compelled to advise the Viscountess of the financial difficulties in which the Baronetcy has fallen. She assured me that she understood completely the obligations I have faced and that it surely was to my credit that I had endeavoured so hard and for so long to maintain it in the appropriate manner.

I assured her that my interest in her daughter had nothing to do with Miss Carteret's own financial situation and Lady Dalrymple assured me that she had not given that idea the least consideration as she has observed complete propriety in all my actions.

Miss Carteret is not, I will admit, a particularly handsome woman and she does have certain aspects that I might normally have bristled at. Over time, though, I have come to discover that she is a fine and healthy woman in all respects. I count myself fortunate that when I did propose to her that she, truly of her own will, accepted my terms.

So, Dearest Daughter, you must congratulate me, your old, decrepit father. Given the physical distance between us and the fear that your remaining in England, in London or at Kellynch Lodge I do not know, might be even more prolonged, we will be marrying in the church that is part of Astings and then plan on ourselves traveling, with Lady Dalrymple, to Bath for an extended stay. We expect that you and Lady Russell will be able to join us there at Laura Place.

We are also anticipating visits there from Anne and Mary, of course, but I most look forward to again seeing you and you seeing me and your own good friend who <u>as of now</u> still remains merely Miss Elinor Carteret.

Father

When I told Lady Russell this wonderful news, she seemed genuinely happy, particularly after I assured her that Elinor is truly the finest of women.

I received a letter this morning from Anne. She says she and her husband can be expected any day. The order had come directing that Frederick's *HMS Anne*—which she revealed is the *Boyne*—to Plymouth and the crew paid off and the boat set aside for who knows what. For that, she was assured that she and her husband will travel to Kellynch within a day or two of their arrival, which I imagine may have happened by the time I received her letter.

Anne asked that I show the letter to Lady Russell, and that fine woman was most excited when she read it. Perhaps it is in part that she will be reunited with my more-favoured sister but even then I believe her view of me has improved during the course of our recent intimacy.

She and I agreed that the Wentworths would likely be staying at the Hall itself since it is where his sister resides— and there is quite ample room there—and expect that we will be called upon to visit it in short order. I am glad the Crofts paid their own visit to me before Lady Russell and I traveled to London. But I trust that Anne and Frederick will visit me as well at the Lodge just as soon as they are able.

This afternoon Admiral Croft and his wife came to see me. They did not remain long but seemed to enjoy the tea and cakes that Lady Russell provided to them. Mrs. Croft said she had received that day a letter from her brother, echoing what Anne told me. So we, the four of us, were quite satisfied about the sudden turn of events.

A nne has arrived to visit Lady Russell and me at the Lodge, with her Captain, They will be staying at the Hall itself with the Crofts.

I cannot say how changed Anne is now that she is Mrs. Frederick Wentworth. She remains in many, perhaps most, ways *Anne*. Yet, she seems less brooding and less...judgmental. And far more happy and pleasant to be with. I do not feel she is forever disapproving of what I am doing, *whatever it might be*. That is all I will say.

It has been said that *all's well that ends well* and it appears now having seen her that it has ended well for her, and I confess to having some jealousy about it.

She was particularly courteous and proper in coming to visit me at the Lodge and inviting me to visit her at the *Hall* whenever I so desire. Lady Russell and I have been there several times and have been treated most appropriately and deferentially—my flower gardens were kept very well, for which I am most gratified—by the tenant of the Baronetcy's great house. It cannot be truly *great* again until Father is restored to its possession, though I did not say that!

As to Anne, she is most solicitous of me. She asks about me and Father and what we did while she was away. She knows from letters I sent of the financial condition that caused me to leave Father in Ireland and of the limited success we seemed to have had with that lawyer in London.

Now, she engages in a regular correspondence with Father and in what he writes to me he too appears to have seen and to be pleased by Mrs. Frederick Wentworth, perhaps even more than he ever was with Miss Anne Elliot!

Oh I cannot say how happy I am. I received Father's letter confirming that the marriage ceremony took place at Astings and there is now a new Lady Elliot. The wedding was held on the tenth of the month and I could not wait to pass the news, especially to Anne and Lady Russell.

We had one of the grooms ride to Uppercross Cottage to inform Mary and leave her to decide how the Musgroves and her sisters-in-law are to be informed.

Friday, October 20, 1815

With the return of Anne, there has been a steady flow of visiting, although I have limited myself to only two or three to Uppercross and one to Mary in her little cottage. Anne has visited Henrietta, now Mrs. Hayter, some ways further from Uppercross in the Crofts' little gig but I see no reason to join her, though I might if it were not so very distant.

I was impressed, I will say, when Mr. and Mrs. Hayter came with Captain and Mrs. Benwick from Uppercross, where they are staying, to the Lodge to visit Lady Russell and me before they continued on to the Hall. They are sweet enough girls, but still are *girls* even after being married and I was not sorry after they were gone.

Then tonight, the Crofts organized a party for all the people recently arrived in the neighbourhood. It was also to have something of a celebration about the recent happy news from Ireland about Father and Elinor. They each, *in absentia*, received a fine toast and then they received one as a couple. The news was perhaps preordained to arrive just in time to be celebrated at the ball.

The Musgroves, the Hayters, the Benwicks, and several others. I was most gratified when I arrived with Lady Russell to be given preference of status over all, and I stood with the Crofts and Anne and Frederick to greet everyone as they arrived. It was a simple enough task, but I found it most fulfilling receiving, chiefly as Father's proxy, the condescension of those who came to the Hall. I was told many times how they hoped to see Father shortly *now that he has such pleasant news*. Father's marriage to the woman who was Miss Carteret and now is *Lady Elliot!* is well known throughout Kellynch. It grieves me to recall the last woman to carry that name was Mother but I am most pleased that it has been taken after these years by a worthy woman of whom I have become most fond and not by some old, deceptive wench who I have come, naturally and with more than enough justification, to abhor and revile.

Indeed, as I was preparing to go this evening, that thought passed across me and for a moment I feared that *she* and, worse, the HP would join the festivities, but I was spared that humiliation. To the contrary, I took some satisfaction in knowing that word of Father's marriage will have reached the HP at least through his mistress from Mr. Shepherd and expect any certainty he had in thinking the title was safe for him has been set aside.

He knows Father is a most virile man and fully capable of siring his own heir and that Elinor—Lady Elliot!—is more than capable of carrying him.

As I say, he made no appearance and with God's grace he shall never pollute Kellynch Hall. I have, however, been largely successful in putting thoughts of him to the side and I will do so now with, as I will in a moment reveal, my own certainty that I will succeed.

Instead, I will speak of the far more pleasant events of this evening and of the pleasant people who *did* appear.

Mostly I will speak of a particular pleasant person—and *particularly* pleasant person—who increased his acquaintance with me and induced me to join him for several dances though I declined all other offers except from my brothers-in-law, Frederick and Charles Musgrove. I believe my preference may have been noticed but I care not.

I refer to Captain Marston. In his finest garb, I will say that his plain scar may have even enhanced his handsomeness, for I cannot deny that he is a most handsome man. And, to use a word applied moments ago to my dear father—perhaps inappropriately by his *daughter*—very virile. I can only wonder why he has not found a woman to whom he could surrender his heart. Perhaps it is due to his now expired commitment to the Navy.

It may sound cruel, but perhaps a benefit of peace will be his turning his interest to establishing a house and a household on *terra firma* as Frederick appears to be doing with Anne and Captain Benwick with Louisa Musgrove. I hope that in one respect he is not like Frederick. That he did not lose his heart when he was young to a woman he was unable, try as he might, to forget.

I go too, too far. I find him, as I fully admit, a most handsome creature. He is polite and proper and his wit and charm seem *genuine*. He says he will be remaining in the neighbourhood as guests of the Crofts, via Frederick, for at least a fortnight and I assured him that I would be happy to stroll with him as we did in London. He has assured *me* that he would be pleased should Lady Russell prove herself unavailable when we do!

I feel like a young and naïve girl and perhaps in part I am, never having had the opportunity before. I am quite happy to be such and I am anxious about whether Captain Marston will be as good as his word about coming to visit in the morning.

How it was raining when I awoke. The water was bashing against my windows very loudly through the curtains. When I heard it, I dropped back on my bed, clutched my blankets tighter to myself, and cursed the weather.

When I did rise and before I went down to eat with Lady Russell, I looked at what I wrote only last night. All this talk of my *heart* I believe now is most unusual for me. As I think on it, though, I will not alter it for I believe that be it my situation or the intervention of Captain Marston or some combination of those two things—and perhaps others including the pleasingness I find in Anne with Frederick and the news from Ireland—that I am myself *altered* since those dark days when I began this Journal. So I will not alter a word of what I wrote even if it shows me as being a foolish and naïve woman.

*   *   *   *

On the way home from the party at the House last night, I had told Lady Russell about Captain Marston's suggestion about visiting on the morrow. This morning, when I went down for breakfast after writing the above, she could not resist teasing me about *the Lord having other plans for my day.* I was not in a humour to hear this from her. My spirits were lifted, though, when not long after we had finished our breakfasts the sun appeared and the air seemed cleansed. The weather, in short, was hardly enough to deter a motivated sailor from venturing to the Lodge to visit, for it is not a great distance. I will admit that one benefit of having come in contact so suddenly with so many naval men is that it has softened my view of such creatures at least as individuals and, in some cases, to have enhanced it!

Within the hour I was proved right: while I *happened* to be gazing down the lane in the direction of the Hall, I saw him and I was up to greet him as he stepped to the door. He sat briefly with Lady Russell and me, before he offered to take us both out for a turn. Lady Russell declined, claiming there was some correspondence she *must take care of* but insisting that her inability not prevent me from going, and of course I did go.

I cannot say that I ever had a more pleasant walk with a man and *I know* I have not had a more interesting one. He queried me as we went along a fine but muddy path that ran across the top of the ridge. It is a favoured stretch for people to walk from the Lodge to the village, but we saw no one. The ground was still quite damp and in spots there were large puddles nearly blocking our way through. But I found I did not care for the muddying of the hem of my dress and I am certain that my companion did not even notice it, though he was quite gallant in helping me when we encountered particularly muddy patches. (I do not envy Bridget, who will have to clean it for me.) His questions were quite appropriate and he had a manner that seemed to invite me to speak more expansively than I might otherwise and that I have ever, as I say, done with a man before. And he nearly a perfect stranger!

He did not ask, but for some reason I believed I could tell him of some of the financial difficulties that arose over the years as Father sought to maintain the dignity of the Baronetcy. It was, I said, the reason I had returned to Kellynch—he well knew the Crofts were tenants to Father— as I sought with the help of Lady Russell to disentangle some of the issues. He agreed that Father's recent marriage would be a blessing. I assured him that I believe Father's attraction to Elinor is genuine and that there is a great mutuality of affection.

He knew some aspects of my family from dinners and excursions with Anne. I asked him about life during the recent hostilities and he said it was as boring as watching grass grow. *Back and forth. Back and forth*, he said, mimicking the movement with his hands. Anne, he said, was a great blessing to all the officers of the ships on blockade duty. Meetings and dinners amongst the various captains were usually held aboard Frederick's *Boyne* simply because the sight of a pretty young woman is quite the treat for a naval man on blockade duty.

He told me things about Frederick I had no idea about, especially about their mutual adventures chasing down privateers and French naval ships attempting to run the prior blockade. That, he said, was where Frederick made much of his fortune. He said very matter of factly that he was not quite so fortunate about prize money but had made enough to make for a pleasant life ashore now that—we all pray—the war is over and done with once and for all.

At some point, perhaps when he finished his pantomime about the mundaneness of blockade duty, I placed my arm through his and there it rested for the balance of our walk.

Frederick, he said, went to sea very young, as a midshipman. His brother-in-law, the Admiral, helped him gain a position on board a vessel and from there he moved up and was fortunate to be given his own command, the *Asp* he said it was, after he earned the rank of post-captain. He and Frederick and the others were like King Henry's Band of Brothers, sometimes stationed near one another, sometimes being sent hither and thither at the Admiralty's whims.

He said Captain Harville—about whom I have heard much but who has yet to be introduced to me—suffered a wound from a mast's splinter that was the result of a French sniper's round and how Captain Benwick—now married to Louisa Musgrove—had lost the love of this life while he was at sea.

"It is something we all fear, that we will be forced to leave someone we love behind and neither they nor we know if we will ever come over the horizon again." He said he vaguely knew of Frederick's early offer to Anne, which she rejected, and that the refusal seemed to haunt him. "He was never one for the harbour wenches," he said. He maintained that neither was he!

He had no love of the sort Frederick had for Anne, though he said his friend hid it quite well from all of comrades. The announcement of their engagement came as quite a surprise. Perhaps it was the peace that did it. Or at least what they thought was the peace only last year. "A sailor in a war would do well not to become entangled lest he leave a widow to survive on a slight pension from the King."

It is something I have heard Lady Russell mention late at night when she has spoken about her changed view of Anne marrying Frederick. She said it was a concern that she used to persuade my sister to reject him the first time, some nine years ago.

I asked Thomas whether his view might have since changed with this latest peace. He said he "feared" he was too old a salt to have changed much. "Wentworth apparently long loved your sister. I have no such advantage with such a woman." He added that having met Anne, she could understand why Frederick long and constantly loved her.

I saw him smile on saying that and I nodded. And thus did he unknowingly answer my concern about the availability of his heart to—I will say—*me*. That it, unlike Frederick's, his bore no restraints from a long-ago, never to be forgotten affection!

Things were quite somber when he spoke of these things until I reminded him that Frederick's constancy had been rewarded and that both he and Anne had fully paid for their bit of *stupidity*, as I poorly put it.

Aye, he said, and Benwick, who I had learned from Anne had lost the one who had taken his heart while he was at sea but had found Louisa Musgrove for himself, he seems to be happy enough.

On that note, we continued our walk and directed our conversation into calmer or at least safer waters. We shortly found ourselves approaching the Lodge. I suggested he come inside to again see Lady Russell, but he declined, pleading a need to get back to the Hall. And with a bow, he was gone.

I go on too long regarding this conversation. But it was such a peculiar and delightful one, even with the sadness we touched upon and the depths we found ourselves in. And when Lady Russell asked about what we spoke, I deferred, claiming it was little more than idle tattle though in my heart I ~~think~~ know it was more than that.

Pleasing as my stay has been here, we must prepare to go to Bath to see Father and *Lady Elliot*. Whether Thomas goes with us and Frederick to Bath or returns to London I do not know.

On a pleasant note, we have received word from Mr. Shepherd that matters are well in hand with Mr. Dumpkin in London to resolve a significant number of matters concerning the Baronetcy as he promised he would—aided I am sure by the improvement in finances that followed Father's wedding—so my view of the lawyer is not as harsh as it was during and immediately after our first meeting.

It has been settled. The group of us will go to Bath to see Father and Lady Elliot. I will stay with Lady Dalrymple—and Father and Elinor. Anne and Frederick will lodge with Lady Russell. Captain Marston will be forced to fend for himself if he cannot fit in there! He is coming, and I would be lying if I did not say that I am excited about what seems such a simple thing.

Navy men seem so different from any I have known before. I knew little about it, but Anne explained how a boy is sent to sea very young. He does not go to Eton or Harrow or the like even if he is in our sphere—though the eldest sons of such families rarely are sent to the sea.

They try not to cry and hope to graduate from being midshipmen to lieutenants and then to passing a rigorous examination to become a post-captain and get themselves on the Navy List. Once there, they can, if ambitious *and lucky*, have the chance of making their fortune as they slowly but irreversibly move up until they may become admirals, as Admiral Croft did as well as that yellow admiral I met at Lady Dalrymple's.

Anne said that in reality it was not so simple but that she was fortunate while on board because they never found themselves involved in any real action. She heard the stories, she said, of how brutal and heartless a naval battle can be.

She told me what Frederick said about how Thomas got his scar. He had never told me, though I had never, now that I think of it, asked. I was wildly curious about it but it would have been wholly impertinent to ask. It was, Anne said, when Thomas's ship and a French one were side by side in the Year Seven when he was a mere lieutenant. The boats were bound together with rope and he turned just quickly enough to avoid the full force of a French sword but not quickly enough to avoid having it create the gash on his face that is so prominent now. Apparently it was very bloody but he remained at his post until the battle was won.

I looked at Thomas differently after this intelligence, though I did not tell him what Anne had said. And I wondered whether he would ever have told me the truth about how it came to be.

I am again diverted. I wish to note that we have scheduled our trip to Bath. I received a letter from Father with express instructions that I share it with Anne and with Lady Russell. It was simply that he was very much in anticipation of our reuniting after so long a separation. It is somewhat unlike what I expect to hear from him, but I am pleased to have received it, as were Anne and Lady Russell.

We have arrived in Bath and I have been made most comfortable at Lady Dalrymple's. I am somewhat disturbed or at least *disappointed* that Captain Marston in the end did not accompany us. This very morning, he announced that he was required to travel to London on a matter of some personal business and that he greatly regretted this.

He was gentleman enough to approach me after the news was delivered to the others to very quietly say he was particularly disappointed about this turn of events and that it was a matter that could not be avoided. While we prepared for our travel, he rode into Salisbury where he will get the stage for his long journey. I cannot say if he will write to me or disclose the nature of this business and whether it has been successfully resolved. I desperately hope that he will return to me. Or at least return so that I might see him.

Other than that, it was as enjoyable as a trip over such a distance made in a single day, ending after it was quite dark, could possibly be. We were in Lady Russell's carriage and she, Anne, and Frederick left me at Laura Place before they continued on to Rivers Street.

I was gratified that both Father and Elinor were awaiting me in the foyer. She accompanied me to the very fine room assigned to me and after I had made myself presentable, she accompanied me to the drawing room, where Father and Lady Dalrymple were waiting.

My looks out the rear of the house on the second floor. As it was late and the others had eaten, food was brought to me by Bridget, who had travelled in a separate carriage with several other servants. I was encouraged by Lady Dalrymple herself to partake of it and I will say that it was quite good and replenishing.

And I must retire now. As I said, it has been most gratifying to return to Bath and especially to see Father again. He seemed a decade younger than when I last left him in Ireland and worlds more content than he had been since he last set foot in Kellynch Hall.

The day after we arrived in Bath was eventful. It was cold but not too cold for our group, which would be Anne, Lady Russell, Elinor, and myself, to walk to Milsom Street and thereabouts to gaze into the shop windows and go into one or two. I believe my earlier conversations with Lady Russell have greatly eased her acceptance of Elinor so deeply into Father's life. There are moments when I saw the two *Ladies* engage in conversations that seemed of the most intimate nature.

We ate, joined by Frederick—whose view towards Lady Russell also seems to improve each day, as does hers of him— at Lady Russell's on Rivers Street.

That good woman's house would be out of place on Camden Place, but I believe it suits her and is very tastefully done up. It was a fine meal and much was said about the dinner we were to attend on the morrow with Father and the Ladies Dalrymple and Elliot.

To be sure, the Dalrymple house on Laura Place would fit very well on any of the finer streets of Mayfair itself! The servants are appropriately stiff in a very fine livery and deferential to all who enter. I, as the eldest daughter of "Sir Walter Elliot of Kellynch Hall," am particularly appreciated by all.

It was the finest of Bath society who came. I cannot say I was ever as excited for Father in the congratulations that flowed across him as he stood between his wife and his mother-in-law to greet them.

I was pleased when Elinor took me aside and we were able to further rekindle much of the friendship that we developed when I was in Wicklow. Even Anne, who I called to sit with us, was pleased and I daresay somewhat surprised by the intelligence and charm of the woman who had been so silent and obsequious when she was merely *Miss Carteret*, with little to say when she was anywhere within her mother's hearing.

It was a pleasant evening, made even more so as we were preparing to leave. Father took me to a spot in the library where we could not be overheard. I feared what he might be about to tell me in his seriousness and indeed he removed a paper from an inner pocket that could be a harbinger of some bleak financial tidings.

But no! It was a letter from Admiral Croft that Frederick carried with him and had given him on a hurried and brief visit to Laura Place earlier in the day. In it, the Admiral graciously offered, under the happily altered circumstances of Father's position, to surrender the lease on the Hall and find accommodations elsewhere in Somerset on a mere moment's notice.

Father said he'd spoken to Elinor about it, and she agreed that though it was a great distance from Astings in Ireland, it was the only thing to do, to have the Baronetcy restored to its *proper place* at the Hall.

He has not told anyone else and begs that I maintain the secret until *he* has the opportunity to reveal it. I was quite ecstatic about agreeing! I daresay, though, that it will not come as a particular surprise when he tells the others. And I cannot hide, though for now I must keep it to myself, how thrilled I am that Elliots will again be residents of Kellynch Hall.

Father and Elinor will remain at Lady Dalrymple's in Bath until they can properly return to Kellynch. The rest of us, though, are to return to Somerset. Father is most enthusiastic about his eventual return and I believe Elinor, by whom I mean "Lady Elliot," may be even more excited about becoming the mistress of *her own house* and stepping into the role her mother maintains in County Wicklow. As to that, Frederick will bring a letter expressing Father's appreciation and acceptance of Admiral Croft's offer. Frederick believes it will not be long before arrangements can be made to find a suitable house for the Crofts.

Thursday, November 30, 1815
Kellynch Lodge

We are back in Kellynch. I have become so familiar with staying at the Lodge that it almost would feel like a home for me were it not so near the Hall. I hope that will change and I am perhaps as excited about that prospect as Father and, perhaps, Lady Elliot are. How fine it will be to resume our walking when she does finally arrive.

For now, though, I must content myself with being at Lady Russell's. I expect that we will venture to the Hall often and that there will be dinners with Mary too and with the Musgroves at Uppercross. It is enough that I can have a fine meal alone with Lady Russell in her small room off her kitchen and can retire to the fine room that is again assigned to me, again with the help of Bridget and Sally, who has stayed behind with her own nearby family when we (and Bridget) went to Bath.

We have been in Kellynch for a day and have had the finest tidings from the Hall itself. The Crofts had anticipated Father's acceptance of their offer and have found an excellent location not twenty miles from the Hall with many old sailors not too distant. They will be able to move there just after the first of the year! Anne rushed to the Lodge to give Lady Russell and especially me the news, and I have already written to Father to tell him and dispatched it as an express so he might know and prepare himself and Elinor for the move back to the Baronetcy's Great Hall in a month's time.

As to *young* sailors, or at least those that were not so elderly, I was content when I went to see Anne at the Hall by the appearance of a veritable squadron of them. For Frederick apparently told Captain Harville of our arrival and so he invited that Captain and his wife—leaving it seems the care of their children to a trusted neighbour in Lyme—to join him with Captain and Mrs. Benwick from Uppercross.

They, of course, were largely left to talk of whatever it is naval officers will speak of when they are together, as Anne says they were forever doing during extended dinners while on station in the Mediterranean. Anne and Louisa and Mrs. Harville, who I found a pleasant enough if not particularly well-bred woman who showed the signs of having several children, and I watched the group of them with interest and some amusement and with even greater interest and even greater amusement as they added to the number of ales they enjoyed while they spoke of their adventures.

This morning broke very cold again, with clear skies and a harsh wind. Lady Russell suggested that we take a carriage to the church, and I could not object. Much deference was accorded us when we arrived and took our seats with Anne and the others from the Lodge in the front two pews in front of the lectern. It was, though, very cold and we all stayed bundled up in our coats and hats and gloves throughout the service, which I believe the vicar cut short to allow us, that being every soul in the congregation, to find more warm accommodations.

Which is what Lady Russell and I found when we went to the Hall with the others, with she and I sharing a carriage with Anne and Mary, who had come from Uppercross Cottage so she could see us. We were followed by a carriage carrying the gentlemen of our group and the Crofts and Charles Musgrove.

Supper itself was very finely done. We spent the afternoon in the well heated drawing room playing several different card games and exchanging partners regularly. That is until Mrs. Croft compelled Anne to sit down before the Hall's fine pianoforte, which I fear is well out of tune for not having been used in some time, and play. She did so with such pleasure that even the sour notes that arose from her fingers were enjoyable in the fine room with the fine company.

As dusk comes very early, Lady Russell and I left at about three o'clock to return to the Lodge and I will say that I am most content about how the day went and what it bodes for the future.

I am quite put out by Anne. And Lady Russell as well. They informed me this afternoon when Anne came to visit us that we are all going to Lyme. She did not ask. She just said it was what was going to happen on the morrow.

Lady Russell accepted this without complaint but I did not. It has been many years since I have been there and there was no particular reason I wished to ever go there again. Particularly in December, when all of the amusements have long been shut down.

Anne says she and Frederick are going there to see the Harvilles and that Mary and Charles are going as well so that I must join them. To my surprise, Lady Russell volunteered that she would be delighted to go for the day. Indeed, the light was such that we would have to stay overnight even though it was but seventeen miles away. Anne assures us that she knows of fine accommodations that are open at this time, being the one where she and the others were when Louisa Musgrove had her horrible accident that changed so many lives.

Anne has told me, in confidence, that it was stupidity and not an accident though. That the impulsive girl intentionally jumped from the wall only for Frederick to be unable to catch her in time. In any case, it led to her very unlikely, Anne said, connexion with Captain Benwick.

Be that as it may, it was hardly an inducement for *me* to make the trip. Anne and Lady Russell were adamant that until Father returns in barely over a fortnight, there really is nothing for me to actually do in Kellynch and I might as well join the others on the trip. I was assured that I would be made comfortable on the way and once we are there, and, in the end, I agreed to go.

Which we will be doing in the morning. It will be six of us and I believe we women at least will huddle together for warmth as we go.

I confess that last night was the most enjoyable I have spent in I do not know how long, perhaps only exceeded by the great and frankly unexpected pleasures of earlier in the once we had arrived by the sea in a cold and desolate Lyme.

I am writing this early the following morning as I was far too tired last night to do anything put fall contentedly into my bed and nest beneath the thick blanket afforded to me by our inn.

Our trip down was quite cold. It was fortunate that we could utilize one of the Musgroves' larger carriages. In addition to me, we were Lady Russell, Anne and Frederick, and Mary and Charles. We alternated places several times along the way, as we changed horses but I will say our closeness served us well by helping to warm us.

Charles and Frederick sat beside one another for much of the trip and spoke of hunting and various other manly pursuits while we women spent the hours on more important—to us— matters!

Although Mary was at first...Mary, as we continued she seemed to relax her anxieties and cease her complaints in the knowledge that her boys were safe at Uppercross with her in-laws and that, indeed, there was the prospect that the Crofts would be joining the Musgroves there for dinner. I cannot say whether that happened, but the idea seemed to please the others quite much. Her boys are very fond of the Admiral, I will say that.

The past is prologue, it is said, and I could not have been more pleased when we actually arrived in the largely empty seaside town. All of its attractions were gone. Only a few inns were open, including the finer one Anne mentioned and where we are staying.

When we were through the door of that establishment, I at first could not believe it. There, sitting in the tavern itself, sat two officers, and Frederick rushed to join them, it being clear that they were waiting for our arrival.

Two? Indeed for my dear Captain Marston was right there with Captain Harville. Mrs. Harville sat at a small table nearby and they were all near the roaring fire.

They all rose and we had a very fine reunion. As fate would have it, when we all sat, I found myself between Lady Russell and Thomas at a sofa set at an angle to the fire. Warm refreshments were promptly brought to us and I fear I largely ignored the others in my attentions to Thomas, though I will credit Lady Russell for being quite encouraging in my conversation with him. If I did not know better, I would think that she and Anne may have been playing some sort of trick on me in getting me to Lyme.

That did not matter. It was cold but not too cold to walk down to the Cobb, which I remember from a trip I took with my parents and sisters perhaps twenty years ago. Though it was warm and sunny that long ago day and we made the trip down and back in a single day.

The wind was rough at times, and I found myself anchored—it is perhaps called—to Thomas with my arm tightly through his as we went. But it was too cold and it was not long before we were back in the inn's tavern re-warming ourselves and planning our evening.

But the evening had been planned. We would be having dinner all together in the inn's large room on the first floor and then the furniture would be placed to the side and the pianoforte pulled away from the wall and we would have a dance.

I need not go into the particulars. Anne played the pianoforte and the informality and familiarity of our group was worlds apart from the dances I have attended even in the limited society of Kellynch and Uppercross. Lines and boxes were formed as necessary and country dances and scotch reels and even a cotillion I did not know were had. I believe I made myself quite the fool in trying the unfamiliar and in the company I did not care particularly that I was likely being made fun of, or at least *some* fun of, by the others. It did not matter. I enjoyed twisting and turning with each of the gentlemen in our party, mixed in with frequent gulps of the punch that was on hand.

And when it was done and we were all exhausted, we retired to our rooms. I missed having Sally and Bridget but was adequately tended to by a local girl at the inn. It was not long before I got myself into that fine bed. I had no time to attend to this Journal. I had to wait till this morning to do so. And now, having completed that task, I must prepare for breakfast. We have been promised a final walk here this morning and then back to Kellynch we go. I shall miss this place, a place to which I gave scant thought for so many years.

*   *   *   *

It was still light out when we reached Kellynch and settled in our respective abodes. I was greatly displeased that Thomas had not accompanied us as he chose to remain with the Harvilles for some days.

I was greatly pleased, however, that when we entered the Lodge's foyer to find two letters for me and one for Lady Russell. Father had written to each of us and Elinor to me. When we were settled, we adjourned to her drawing room near the great fire—it did take some time and some hot confections to warm ourselves adequately—and in our chairs at an angle to one another and in the light of some candles, we each read what was written to us.

Father's, I must say, was quite simple. Arrangements were being made for his arrival *with his wife Lady Elliot* for two or three days after the new year began. He very much looked forward to seeing me and especially to resuming his position in Kellynch itself. He asked that I advise the others of his expected arrival, though he insists that he has no expectations of any but the most simple of greetings from the family or the neighbourhood.

Lady Russell laughed when I pointed this passage out to her, saying he had said much the same to her, absurd as we both knew it to be.

Lady Elliot's letter, though, was of an intimacy I had not as yet felt with her. I do not know how else to speak of it and so I again am copying it here, neglecting some of the mundane details concerning her planned trip.

Laura Place
Bath

15 December

My Dear,

I hardly know what to call you. You are, of course, my "dear" but it does not sit right with me to call you anything but "Elizabeth" and I would much prefer it if I remain "Elinor" to you—at least when we are alone or with friends.

What I do know is that my anticipation of coming finally to Sir Walter's much loved estate increases by the day. I feel it must be some sort of present awaiting my arrival so that I may open it and take possession. I have heard so much about it from you but even more from your dearest Father that my only fear is that its reality will not reach the heights of my expectations about it. Indeed, I do not know that it could. Half of it, I am certain, will be more than adequate for someone who cares far more for its custodian and ~~his~~ my fine family.

I shall, you know, be dependent on you to teach me the proper way to be Lady Elliot. I can never take the place of your dearly loved Mother. I assure you that I have not done so, or attempted to do so, with your Dear Father. I am who I am as your Mother was who she was. I can only hope to do some small credit to her memory and continue the maintenance of Kellynch Hall in the manner that she and later that you did.

It is a joyous time. It will only be made more so when I am finally back with you, my dear Elizabeth.

Elinor

Lady Russell left me alone as I read. I could not shield the tears that flowed with each word, written in that neat hand that I first saw in the invitation she scrivened on her mother's behalf to invite us to visit Astings. The reality that Father and Elinor would soon be home, for it is clear that Elinor now considers Kellynch *her* home, brought emotions upon me that I could not have imagined.

Lady Russell and I spoke about it later but only in the most general terms. I believe, however, that she has become more than pleased by Father's selection and that she, too, is beginning to feel excitement about his and Elinor's coming.

I thought I was exhausted last night from the dancing. I believe I am even more so now, from the travel and especially from the news from Bath. I am back in my own room—at the Lodge at least—and will soon be falling very happily into my own bed.

As the Crofts will soon be leaving the Hall, we looked forward to spending Christmas Day there even in Father's absence. It was important as a thanks for their kindness in agreeing to leave so Father could properly return.

It was a rather large group. Those from Uppercross, joined by Mr. and Mrs. Benwick, attended services in the church there, with Mr. Hayter doing the honours, while we from the Hall and the Lodge were content at the far smaller Kellynch Church. A grand supper was prepared at the Hall. When the Musgroves and the others from Uppercross arrived, Admiral Croft reigned over our meal and celebration, with the various children, young and old, racing around the place and putting all of us in fear that some damage might be done! But in the event, none was, and we left the Hall in quite the condition that it was in when we arrived.

Oh Joy! Thanks to the efficiency of a pair of Navy men—being Admiral Croft and Captain Wentworth—and two Navy *women*—Mrs. Croft and *Mrs.* Wentworth—all of the Crofts' belongings were loaded onto wagons shortly after we all entered a new and, we hope, more peaceful year.

And thanks to that, Father arrived back *at the Hall* late this afternoon. In the anticipation of this, I have moved my things into my old room there. There was much other moving about. Anne and Frederick's things have been moved to the Lodge.

Thomas arrived at the Lodge in the early afternoon, quite frozen I believe from his ride from Lyme. He will be staying there for at least a fortnight with Anne and Frederick (and Lady Russell). I was beyond excitement when, unbeknownst to me beforehand, he arrived with Lady Russell, Anne, and Frederick at the Hall from the Lodge to await Father's arrival.

Were I an articulate writer, I do not know that I could do justice to how pleased we all were at Father's appearance with the new Lady Elliot. Though it was cold, a groom was assigned to a place on a slight hill that was to the north of the Hall. It gave him a view through the bare trees of the road to Kellynch. We were all in anticipation—by which I mean Anne and Frederick, Lady Russell, Thomas, Mary and Charles, and even Mr. and Mrs. Musgrove, and me, of course—as the sun began its winter descent. There was much pacing, I can say, until Charles turned from the window to announce that the groom was racing towards us.

And then before we knew it, we could see the approach of the carriage and four with its single coachman and pair of footmen at the rear, all in heavy coats and thick gloves and ear-covering caps. Even before it halted in front, we rushed through the front door. It was cold, as I say, and we did not dawdle and how I hugged Elinor, and she waited for Father and the pair of them wasted little time in crossing back into the Hall. We were quite glad of that. After a review of the servants who were lined up in the foyer, we convened in the sitting room, all silent in anticipation of what Father would say.

He looked around the room as he and his Lady warmed themselves and at each of us in turn and at the fire and pronounced himself "very pleased indeed" to be back and "very pleased as well" as to the condition of the Hall upon his initial view of it. His eyes set upon Thomas, who he did not know.

Frederick immediately introduced him to Father as well to Lady Elliot. Father, I fear, fell back at his prejudices against the Navy when he could not avoid seeing the scar—he was at least diplomatic enough not to mention it. As to Elinor, I had not mentioned him in our correspondence for fear, I believe, that nothing would come of it. Upon seeing him, after a moment of reflection, she turned to me and gave the slightest bit of a smile before turning back and saying how very pleased she was to meet him and I truly believe she was.

It was late, and we had dinner not long after they arrived. There was little opportunity to converse with either Father or Elinor, although she told me how pleased she indeed was to see me and Thomas and the Hall itself, saying she was truly humbled by what had happened to her. And she made me promise that whatever weather appears in the morning— within reason—on the morrow, we shall resume our habit of taking walks together and that I am to show her my favourite places on the estate.

I am tired and it is late and my bed beckons me with Bridget having left. Thus I must be brief.

We all, except for Father, who said he was too tired for an evening of reverie, went to celebrate Twelfth Night at the old mansion at Uppercross. I believe that Elinor was somewhat anxious about making the trip there but I assured her that the Musgroves were very fine if old-fashioned people and that she would be most welcome. We went in a pair of carriages, one from the Hall, one from the Lodge, and I sat with Elinor, Anne, and Lady Russell for the trip.

As I knew they would be, the Musgroves were exceedingly pleased to see *Lady Elliot* again. When we were settled, we each selected a Shakespearean character from bags—one for the ladies, the other for the gentlemen—for our night's persona. And who should I select but Lady Macbeth? I was matched to Frederick's King Macbeth itself.

Toil and trouble indeed!

Oh how Anne laughed at that as she became Portia and Lady Russell Ophelia. Thomas was Romeo but his Juliet was Mary. Oh how Charles cringed at that until he became Hamlet and insisted on accompanying Lady Russell for much of the night!

It was a fine meal but seeing as how the great house is far from town, we did not enjoy the pleasures of wassailing but had food and drink enough to keep us all warm and content until it was time to leave. We rolled back in the same configuration as we had rolled there. Elinor and I came into the foyer not half-an-hour ago and I am far too tired and lushy to continue this until tomorrow when my recollection of events might be improved.

Although Charles Hayter is the rector at Uppercross, and Mary attends Sunday services there, the rest of us went to the familiar Kellynch Church. It was a cold morning, though with the prospect of a bright sun warming things up in the afternoon. Father, Elinor, and I departed the Hall to walk. Elinor told him it would be sad not to enjoy a walk on the estate. And it was not a long walk in any case, surely not long enough to justify taking one of the carriages unless the weather advised against it. We were very bundled up. As we approached, we could see Lady Russell, Anne and Frederick, and to be sure *Captain Marston* waiting outside, each of them rocking slightly side to side and rubbing their gloved hands in their various attempts to try to warm up. Indeed the gentlemen's ears were quite pink by the time we reached them.

It is a small church with a small congregation. It was perhaps even colder inside than out, but not too cold to follow the protocols for the service. I cannot say how gratified Father was when, upon entering this simple building after so long an absence, the entire congregation rose in his honour and watched as he and the new Lady Elliot stepped slowly and regally down the aisle, with Lady Russell and me following them and Anne and the two Captains behind us as we filled the first two rows in front of the lectern.

Once the sound of the congregants resuming their seats in the pews had stopped echoing about the place, the vicar came out. He is old and long familiar to us. Before beginning his other duties, he stepped to the front pew and bowed to Father, who rose to greet him. They exchanged pleasantries in the otherwise silent church until he stepped back and lifted his arms, the signal for the balance of the churchgoers to rise and begin the first hymn.

I cannot recall what hymns were sung or what readings were read or what was said in the sermon as I was too aware of a certain gentleman in the row behind me. He and the others who accompanied us back to the Hall at a somewhat hurried pace given the very chilled air and what a relief it was that fine fires had been set in both the dining parlour and the sitting room and a fine meal was brought to us, the combined occupants of Kellynch Hall and Kellynch Lodge and it was delightful to be back.

I cannot say how delightful today has been. After the cold on Sunday, the weather turned completely and while the sun was still out and bright, the temperature was far above what it was, so much so that walking in a simple dress beneath a light coat and wearing gloves and a fine bonnet was manageable.

As the Lodge is not far and I was up earlier than usual, I ventured after breakfast to walk in that direction. I wanted to see if Anne was perhaps of a mind to join me to walk along a favourite grove. I have become far fonder of walking than in prior days, and I count my excursions with Elinor in Wicklow and Dublin and with Lady Russell in Kellynch and London amongst my finest recent memories. They are pleasant respites from whatever is vexing me and I expect I will enjoy the pleasures from often doing the same with Anne.

I did not actually arrive, however, because when I was within sight of Lady Russell's, a fine figure was heading towards me. In a moment I realised it was Thomas himself, walking easily with a switch swinging in his right hand as his left removed his hat when he saw me. Upon exchanging greetings, he said he was most pleased to have "happened upon" me. "Will you take me," asked he, "on some of your favoured walks?" I am quite familiar with almost every inch of the neighbourhood from my long being an inhabitant and was delighted to fulfill his request.

Oh how he allowed me to prattle on about this tree and that bush. A brook runs along the side of a grove to the east of the Lodge, and we stopped at it. It was hurrying across the stones on the bottom, gurgling now and then and looking very, very cold. I asked if it has any resemblance to the sea.

There was a large rock set across the path from the water that had the benefit of being in the sun, and he led me to it. It is a favourite place to stop to recover when a hint of fatigue set upon me. He paused and then said that he had known icy water and water that was nearly steam it was so warm. He'd been part of a squadron that crossed over to the Canadas in the recent war with America and feared for any of his crew that went overboard. "They could not long survive so far north," he said, and I shuddered at the thought. He assured me happily that none did.

"Yet I have also been to the West Indies in the summer with the sun baking us and I sometimes feared for anyone falling in there lest he be boiled alive."

"Really?" I asked.

"No, Miss Elliot," he laughed. He said the water is very warm but not boiling and more than a few times his crew dove in to enjoy the Caribbean's warmth. The natives there were quite amiable, he said, except for the slaves, whose lives they could all see were very hard and they also heard that conditions for them could be barbaric.

I was taken aback by the vehemence of what he was saying but, having no experience in the matter—I thank God—I remained silent. He seemed to recover himself quickly, and I ventured to ask about what life was aboard one of the King's warships.

I had given little thought to this. Of what provisions they had and how they slept and how they tolerated being atop one another. I asked whether the crewmen were naked when they did this swimming about and he laughed again, "Of course, as was I," and I must say I believed I turned quite scarlet at the idea.

I cannot truly say whether it was the consequence of the natural motion of his laughing but I found his hand to have lowered itself to my leg—though he did immediately remove it and became very proper and stoic and though we were comfortable enough sitting on that boulder, he rose and suggested we resume our turn.

I was most affected by this innocent encounter with him and neither of us spoke much beyond him asking, quite genuinely, about life as the eldest daughter of a Baronet whose Mother passed young.

We too soon found ourselves approaching the Lodge. Anne must have seen us for she came out to inquire where the two of us had been and she seemed not the least bit satisfied with my explanation of having simply shared a quiet walk with one another while I undertook my *duty* of showing her visitor the trees and boulders and such things in the area. She offered to have us come inside for some tea, but we declined and Thomas accompanied me back to the Hall and Anne remained at the Lodge and when he left me, I sat with a novel I largely ignored until it was time to dress for dinner with Father and Elinor. It will be some days, I believe, before they are ready to send out invitations to others to dine at the Hall. These initial nights with only the three of us will be, I hope, extremely pleasant and intimate to us all. This first one was very much that to me.

I fell ill, though hardly deathly so, soon after my recent visit *almost* to the Lodge. I cannot say if it was the result of the walk with Thomas but as I am recovered, I can confirm that if that was the price to be paid for that delightful hour it was well worth it.

Anne was tending to me as I daresay only Anne can tend to someone, and when we were alone, she told me about him. I did not inquire about him. To be clear, I did not *object* when she volunteered to tell me and I know I was foolish not to have inquired earlier so I might have avoided falling in love with someone I did not truly know.

Captain Thomas Marston is the son of an earl, though not the first son. He had never told this to me. His father is the Earl of Charlbury in Oxfordshire, and he is the third son, sent off to the Navy when he was twelve. He, according to Anne—and I must think from Frederick—had a rough upbringing and more ran away to the Navy rather than was sent to it. She could not say when he last visited the family estate or when he had even communicated with his father.

It is quite an unfortunate situation, being estranged from one's own father. I could not imagine it, particularly knowing the pain that I felt with the death of Mother. He has no chance of inheriting anything, the heir apparent of that title already having two sons and he, Thomas, having two older brothers. He also has a younger sister of whom Anne knew very little beyond that she remains unmarried.

During my brief confinement while I was ill, the man himself accompanied Frederick to inquire about my condition and I was presentable enough on the third day to receive the two officers in the sitting room, with Anne and Elinor as my vigilant watchers.

These visits were brief and uneventful, but no less precious for that and the moment he left I longed for the next one. I must admit that I have come to love him.

There were moments yesterday when I stared at what I had written the day before and stared at it again and even thought to strike it or even rip up the page on which it was put down and throw it into the small fire in my room. I even may have reached to do that more than once. But I never did.

At the same time, I did not go outdoors lest the object of my affection come to visit while I was out. He has never visited without accompanying Anne and Frederick. On one visit, I found myself cloistered with him when Elinor stepped out and my sister and brother-in-law seemed to find something else in the room to draw their interest and it was very pleasant to be near him again!

He did not come, alone or otherwise, yesterday. The sun set early and only the three of us dined together. Elinor has, I will say, done well on Father's countenance and spirits and I cannot say his dignity has been in the least bit diminished by his being…happy.

That was yesterday and will quickly disappear in light of today's events. It was very cold so we took a carriage to the church. As they did last Sunday, those from the Lodge waited for our arrival outside, and the congregation rose when we entered until we took our seats. Yet unlike the prior Sunday, Thomas somehow maneuvered so that I found *him* beside me in our pew as the first hymn began.

He looked at me *not once* as he sang—rather poorly but spiritedly I believe—from his hymnal nor at any other point through the entire service. I found this most disconcerting. When we left the church, he was again beside me, helping me to our carriage. As he held out his hand to help me in, he told me he very much looked forward to seeing me at supper.

The Lodge's occupants were intrepid enough to brave the cold back to the Hall—Anne would not allow me to walk with them because of my recent illness—and got there not long after we had discarded our coats and hats and gloves and were recovering some warmth in the sitting room. It was a fine fire we enjoyed and it was not long before the others were with us and we had all thrown ourselves on the various chairs and sofas as servants distributed cups of hot tea and coffee amongst us.

It was a fine supper, as it generally is when Father presides now that he is back at the Hall. He has already made some alterations to the Baronetage, to include his marriage to Elinor Carteret,

> daughter of Viscount—deceased
> 1805—and Viscountess Dalrymple.

And promptly after setting down the foregoing, he wrote immediately after Anne's birthdate:

> Married, April 6, 1815, Frederick
> Wentworth, Captain, Royal Navy.

Because Frederick has no living parents who are, in Father's view, not "nobodies," no mention was made of them, though in truth there was barely enough room for them were it otherwise.

I do not particularly like the volume for other reasons, but I am pleased by these additions.

That is neither here nor there, however, for when I excused myself this afternoon, I met Thomas as I started back to the drawing room where we had all assembled near another of the fires that were necessary to keep the house warm. This encounter was quite like but quite unlike the similar encounter I had in Ireland with that corpulent fellow Lady Dalrymple apparently thought I was destined to marry!

Thomas did not hinder my return to the others except by restraining my heart! I have said it. He spoke quite eloquently but I can scarce recall a word that passed his lips to my ear. All

I recall, all I *need* recall, is that he asked to marry me and I told him I would. In the end, it was as simple as that.

We grasped for each other at the same moment and soon I heard him say—I shall always recall *this*—that he loved me and I may or may not have told him that I loved him though I surely did love him and when he released me, his fingers caressed my cheek and he bent down to kiss me on the lips. Then he pulled back and I found my own fingers tracing that large yet somehow invisible scar that cut across his own cheek and it was resolved.

Not completely, however. When we returned to the drawing room, Thomas walked straight to Father, who stood before him. There must have been some hint of what was to happen as the room fell silent. He was very simple and direct, as one expects a naval man to be, and told Father that he had requested my hand and that I had given it to him and that he hoped he, Father, was pleased by the arrangement and would give it his blessing.

Amongst the room, I believe Father was the only one not to have anticipated this and he was quite flustered at what he was being asked to do.

It did not last long. Yes, he had extended his blessing to Anne's union with Frederick but that was *Anne*. When he looked over at me, though, I nodded. After a slight moment of contemplation—and doubtlessly affected by his having learned at some point that Thomas was the son of an Earl—he extended his hand, quickly taken by the Captain.

And with that, Father's blessing was obtained and hard on its heels came the congratulations of the assembled group.

I cannot say when I will be able to return to this Journal for my life is to change in ways I cannot imagine. The third bann was posted today and on the morrow I am to become Mrs. Thomas Marston. Kellynch Hall is crowded with people preparing for the ceremony. Lady Dalrymple has kindly agreed to attend as have Lord and Lady Charlbury and Thomas's two brothers and their wives and children and his one sister, who is two years younger. They arrived from Oxfordshire three days ago and have been made comfortable, I hope, in the finest guest rooms—except for the one accorded to Lady Dalrymple—in the Hall and I cannot describe how pleased Father is to have such eminence in *his* house.

I cannot say that I am particularly pleased by the presence of the male members of his family. His father in particular appears to be an overbearing type and his brothers are quite full of their own supposed importance, though I cannot understand why, other than, as to the elder brother, Michael, his title. If there is one thing I have come to understand, it is that the title does not make the man but it is the man that makes the title. As Father does the Baronetcy and the HP never could.

Thomas's younger sister, though, is called Margaret and seems a sweet enough woman though she is quite reserved. Thomas tells me that his parents are anxious about her finding an appropriate husband. As she is somewhat pretty, is quite personable once one surmounts her shyness, and has a fair amount for a dowry, I expect that in time she will find such a man and in that case I will be pleased to know them.

I can tell that Thomas remains a disappointment of sorts to the Earl himself. Lord Charlbury is a gentlemanly enough sort, but his distaste for the Navy and for his son lowering himself to marry the eldest daughter of a mere baronet is all too apparent, though he is judicious enough as to Father to hide it.

As to his mother, though, things are far different. She has sat with me several times and has inquired about me and Father in a most kind manner and I believe she has decided that I am quite a proper choice to be her youngest's son's wife.

I can at last say, though, that I care not for that. His father may look down upon me but it is Thomas's beautiful face, scar and all, that *I* hope to always be able to look upon.

In the wonderful aftermath of the wedding, this Journal was misplaced and I only came upon it now and fear I have much to add to the foregoing.

The wedding itself was held at Uppercross because Kellynch Church, for all its memories and the presence in the cemetery of Dear Mother's remains, was too small. It was officiated by Charles Hayter. Anne stood beside me and Frederick stood beside Thomas. The families were there and were joined by all those from Uppercross, including my nephews Charles and Walter Musgrove. The Navy was well represented, including by Admiral and Mrs. Croft and Captains Berwick and Harville and their wives.

Ladies Dalrymple and Russell, of course, as well as Lady Charlbury.

I must comment on that latter woman. I was quite surprised during the ceremony when as part of the process Frederick handed an extraordinary ring to Thomas, and my soon-to-be husband placed it very, very delicately on my finger. Only later did he tell me that his trip to London while I was going to see Father in Bath was in part to meet with his parents, who were in town. He explained his general intent as to me. His father took little interest in the matter, as was his normal view towards his third son. His mother asked question after question about me and about how he truly felt about me. He said her verdict convinced him to make his proposal to me and she confirmed her support by giving one of her finer rings to him to present to me should I agree to become her daughter-in-law.

And with that ring I became a part of his family as well as my own.

He delayed his actual proposal until after Father had returned. That not only showed the proper deference, but it allowed him to immediately get Father's approval of our match, though the law did not require it. As the wedding was held in February, we accepted Lady Dalrymple's invitation to visit Ireland, and so spent time at her estate there and several days in Dublin itself.

And we then took up our lives in Somerset.

Perhaps the greatest of news is that the Baronetage has been restored to its proper place in Kellynch Hall and I no longer either avert my eyes or close that fine book when I come upon it. The words Father put in it long ago—"heir presumptive"—have been stricken most brutally by the very hand that wrote them there in the first place. Another, far more pleasant, phrase has appeared elsewhere in the small print made necessary by the limited space. For after a reference to Father's marriage to Elinor on October 10, 1815:

> by which lady he has issue Walter, Jr., born
> November 5, 1816—heir apparent.

Father received no acknowledgement from the, I will say it, *former* heir presumptive, whose place was so gloriously taken by my new brother! He did *not* marry my former intimate friend—who I will deign as an act of pure charity refer to as "Mr. Shepherd's daughter"—but she was cast off abruptly when he discovered he had placed her in the family way. She with the new baby, a girl, returned to the nearby market town to live with her father and the two children she had abandoned to chase after one Elliot or another. So I am led to understand. For appearance's sake, the former HP gave her some slight settlement and no more has been heard from him. As to her, I cannot avoid seeing her now and then in the little town. I am as cordial as I am required to be. But no more.

While we do regularly travel with Father and Elinor to Bath when Lady Dalrymple is there and are quite content to squeeze ourselves into her house on Laura Place, we have yet to go to London. My desire to do so is far reduced from when it was before I met Thomas, however. Nor do I have the slightest interest now to venture to Paris.

This is particularly the case because of how pleasant our days in Somerset are. We live in a cottage that was built on the Kellynch estate. It is small and suits us quite well. I am most proud of the flower garden that I have grown with cuttings from the one I created at the Hall and I am excited about its condition as we move into the spring. It is where I spend much of my time as a married woman.

Thomas made enough of a fortune to allow us to live comfortably, provided we remain within our means. He and Frederick often ride to Lyme in the Wentworth phaeton to visit and gain some much needed sea air. In Somerset, they go hunting with Charles Musgrove and sometimes with Mr. Musgrove and Charles Hayter as well. Plus visits, with Anne, to Admiral and Mrs. Croft—where they sometimes spend the night before coming back to Kellynch. Indeed, Elinor and I once ventured along on one of the visits, and we found the Crofts quite admirable and I am glad to have had them introduced to me, especially given how well they treated the Hall and especially how they tended to my little garden there.

When the men are gone for several days, I spend my time with Anne, who with Frederick is happily residing at the Lodge with Lady Russell.

Most pleasantly, Father's own *Little Walter* is a handsome chap, though I cannot say as Mary insists that he has the "Elliot countenance." Only time will tell. And if he does not, I can hope that the creature growing in my belly will. Anne, Lady Russell, and I frequently stroll along the familiar paths and are sometimes joined by the new Lady Elliot, all three of us younger women carrying rounded bellies and wondering which of us will be the source of the next Elliot girl.

Finis.

Acknowledgements

I have the generous support of several pre-publication readers who contributed mightily to the final product, although I bear responsibility for the defects with it.

I was fortunate to have many fine people help me as beta readers, for whom I am grateful: Melissa Anne Barbato and Gratia Ip.

The Author

Joseph P. Garland has written numerous stories and several novels. This is his third venture into the world of Jane Austen. He has published three novels set in the early years of the Gilded Age in New York and a contemporary novel set chiefly in New York. He is a New York lawyer.

His books can be found at:
https://dermodyhouse.com/books/

Pride and Prejudice Sequels/Variations

Becoming Catherine Bennet: *A Pride and Prejudice Sequel Of Lizzy, Kitty, and Miss Anne de Bourgh* (on KU) (first chapters)
The Omen at Rosings Park: *How Elizabeth Became Mrs. Darcy* (on KU) (first chapters)

NYC's Gilded Age

Róisín Campbell: An Irishwoman in New York (first chapters)
A Studio on Bleecker Street (first chapters)
A Maid's Life (first chapters)

Contemporary

I Am Alex Locus: **My Search for the Truth** (first chapters)